A G-3 rattled off a burst somewhere to Bolan's left

The Executioner raced across the road, pursued every step of the way by a line of bullets. Seconds later he dived behind the cover of a stand of pines.

He studied the opposite side of the valley as well as he could without exposing himself to enemy fire. As he'd expected, his opponent had a hundred places to hide.

But the warrior had no time to waste. He stood and hurried up the slope toward his companions.

Again bullets from the G-3 raced after him, kicking up clouds of dust. But this time the enemy was shooting to kill.

As much as Bolan hated to face the truth, the evidence was undeniable—the Shadow had switched sides....

MACK BOLAN®

The Executioner

#125 Dead Man's Tale	Stony Man Doctrine
#126 Death Wind	Terminal Velocity
#127 Kill Zone	Resurrection Day
#128 Sudan Slaughter	Dirty War
#129 Haitian Hit	Flight 741
#130 Dead Line	Dead Easy
#131 Ice Wolf	Sudden Death
#132 The Big Kill	Rogue Force
#133 Blood Run	Tropic Heat
#134 White Line War	Fire in the Sky
#135 Devil Force	Anvil of Hell
#136 Down and Dirty	Flash Point
#137 Battle Lines	Flesh and Blood
#138 Kill Trap	Moving Target
#139 Cutting Edge	Tightrope
#140 Wild Card	Blowout
#141 Direct Hit	Blood Fever
#142 Fatal Error	Knockdown
#143 Helldust Cruise	Assault
#144 Whipsaw	Backlash
#145 Chicago Payoff	Siege
#146 Deadly Tactics	Blockade
#147 Payback Game	Evil Kingdom
#148 Deep and Swift	Counterblow
#149 Blood Rules	Hardline
#150 Death Load	Firepower
#151 Message to Medellín	
#152 Combat Stretch	
#153 Firebase Florida	
#154 Night Hit	
#155 Hawaiian Heat	
#156 Phantom Force	
#157 Cayman Strike	
#158 Firing Line	

DON PENDLETON'S
THE EXECUTIONER®
FEATURING MACK BOLAN®

FIRING LINE

A GOLD EAGLE BOOK FROM
WORLDWIDE®

TORONTO • NEW YORK • LONDON • PARIS
AMSTERDAM • STOCKHOLM • HAMBURG
ATHENS • MILAN • TOKYO • SYDNEY

First edition February 1992

ISBN 0-373-61158-7

Special thanks and acknowledgment to
Roland Green for his contribution to this work.

FIRING LINE

There is something about him that even treachery
cannot trust.

—Junius
(fl. 1769)

No amount of experience, no amount of skill and no
amount of self-control can make a man comfortable
with treachery.

—Mack Bolan

To the ceaseless efforts of
the men and women of VICAP

Prologue

Sam Brito was a retired major in the United States Marine Corps. He had a name among snipers, as well as a Distinguished Service Cross, two Silver Stars, a Purple Heart from Vietnam and alimony payments to two ex-wives.

The alimony payments had made him dubious about the cost of renting the blue Pontiac he'd driven down to the waterfront. But if Corporal Goss was on the level, it would be worth it.

Brito hoped that Goss *was* on the level. The Pentagon wasn't happy about rumors that the Silent Brotherhood was recruiting Marines at the Bangor Trident facility. Among other things, those Marines guarded warheads. You didn't want a bunch of right-wing terrorists even thinking about getting access to nukes.

The Pentagon also wasn't happy that rumors were all they had so far. Goss was the first thing they had that might be solid. But the man wouldn't talk to just anybody. It had to be somebody he knew, or at least knew about, like "Brillo" Brito.

The night was windless and the fog clung to the water of Puget Sound as Brito walked onto the pier. The structure itself was on its last pilings, but the bollards were cast-iron, a century old. All those years of exposure to northwestern fog and spray had coated them with rust, but left them sound inside. One of them made a good seat for Brito.

The water lapped at the pilings, and something clunked against one of them, a crate or empty barrel left floating by a sloppy warehouseman or sailor.

Completely invisible in the fog, a boat's motor purred like a giant cat. Brito tried to follow the sound, but the fog and the trees distorted it. He had to admit that his hearing wasn't what it had been, thanks to Vietnam and too many firing ranges.

As the sound of the motor faded, Brito heard footsteps on the landward end of the pier, from the opposite direction to his car, which made him breathe a little easier.

He'd checked the buildings on his way in, in case this whole thing was a setup. He hadn't found a soul, but he'd found several good routes back to his car. He could run them even in the dark and the fog, and lay ambushes if he had to. He'd never kill a man at five hundred yards again, but he was still deadly at fifty, and his legs were a lot better than his hearing.

"Brillo here," he called softly. "Gosling?"

No answer. Maybe he'd called too softly. Brito cupped his hands.

As he did, a thick forefinger mashed a button on the boat out on the sound. A radio signal flashed to the receiving antenna of the floating charge that Brito had heard bumping against the pilings and reached the detonator.

A hundred pounds of explosives shot flame and steel fragments into the air. The heavy timbers of the pier tamped the blast a little, but not enough. The pressure ruptured the wood and hurled it into the air in pieces.

Sam Brito was still alive when he struck the water. He might even have made it to shore if he'd been left alone. But the man who'd made the footsteps raced to where Brito was floundering in the water, aiming an Uzi. When the magazine was empty, the only trace of Brito was the blood in the water. Even that was already fading as the waves from the explosion surged back and forth in the little bay.

The gunman shoved a fresh magazine into his weapon and ran to Brito's car. He laid the Uzi on the seat beside him, hot-wired the ignition and backed the Pontiac out of the driveway. A look at his watch told him that he had plenty of time, even using the back roads to avoid the police or anybody else who couldn't mind their own business. Twenty more minutes, and the car, like Brito, would be history.

1

The name on the ticket read Mike Belasko, but it was Mack Bolan, the Executioner, who boarded the red-eye flight for Seattle at Chicago's O'Hare International.

He slept for most of the flight and awoke only as the plane slid down through the morning fog to Sea-Tac International Airport. He was already fully alert by the time the signs told him to fasten his seat belt.

He'd traveled light, so deplaning was a simple matter of standing up and walking out. But there was nothing simple about what he did after that.

For Bolan, covering his tracks was almost instinctive. He used the airport's ingenious subway system as a starting point for confusing anyone trying to follow him. He popped in and out of the cars at random intervals, and finally ended up back near the gate where he'd deplaned. Seeing no obvious surveillance, Bolan moved on.

The airport limousines were just beginning to run, so he took one to a suburb at least ten miles from his destination. He waited behind somebody's scraggly hedge to see if the limo had been tailed, then cut two miles through the suburbs and a mile after that through undeveloped woodland. Finally he called a taxi from a public phone booth and took it to the safehouse in the Tacoma suburb of Thomas.

The house was a two-bedroom A-frame that had, like its neighborhood, seen better days. But the Taiwanese immigrant who owned it owed his life to the Executioner. The man thought the least he could do to repay him was to offer the house to Bolan for the duration of his stay.

Even though he trusted Dzeng, Bolan still approached the house cautiously. Seeing that everything was okay, Bolan let himself in. The back bedroom held a bed, a desk, two chairs and a Victorian wardrobe the size of a small tank. In the wardrobe's false back the warrior found what he expected: a Weatherby, with a daylight scope sight and an infrared that would let him work effectively at night or in the area's perennial mist and fog; a Beretta 93-R, with a shoulder stock that effectively tripled its range; a .44 Desert Eagle, whose huge slugs could crack an engine block; ammunition for all three, with spare magazines for the Beretta and Desert Eagle; knives, first-aid kit, emergency rations, water purification tablets, dry socks and underwear—a complete kit for surviving, fighting and winning another battle against the lawless.

Bolan checked all three weapons. He found one cartridge that might be defective and a little too much oil on one of the Desert Eagle's magazines.

Otherwise there was nothing to do now for eight hours but check in with Brognola and then get some sleep.

The scrambler on the phone whistled rudely as Brognola came on the line.

"Hal, I've arrived, and everything you sent checked out. The people did a good job."

"I'll pass that along." Brognola sounded subdued. "Somebody else did a good job on Sam Brito last night."

Bolan was silent. Trying to hurry Hal Brognola was a waste of time.

A moment later the big Fed continued. "Either somebody set him up, or there was a leak. He was going for a meet with a source on the Silent Brotherhood, but the Brotherhood crashed the party. Booby trap, then an Uzi. They picked twelve rounds out of the man after they fished him out of the water. I suspect he was supposed to disappear, but somebody didn't read the tide tables."

The warrior frowned. He'd come out to Seattle to join in the fight against the shadowy Silent Brotherhood, a replacement for Brito.

Now the torch had been passed much sooner than anyone had anticipated. The Silent Brotherhood had spoken, in the only language that its kind understood—blood and fear.

The reply would have to be in the same tongue.

"What's your guess, Hal? Setup or bad luck?"

"No evidence either way. Somebody did go over Brito's apartment before the police got there, but it was a sloppy job. Whoever made the hit set the search up fast or used second-rate talent. They missed a couple of things, including a note about a Corporal Goss."

"Marine?"

"Security detachment at the Trident facility at Bangor. He was supposed to have something for Brito."

"Well, he'd better have something for us."

"That might not be as easy as it sounds," Brognola replied. "Goss is missing, too."

"Dead?"

"They have him listed as AWOL, so far."

Bolan nodded. "I think I'd better have a chat with a friendly cop."

"If you can find one. Remember who the chief is now."

The Executioner frowned. The current chief of police in Seattle was a man he'd embarrassed the last time he fought criminals in Puget Sound. The then-commander of the homicide unit hadn't been on the take himself, but he had certainly winked at some officers who were. Bolan wondered how the man's career had recovered enough to let him make it to chief, even if he was only a couple of years short of retiring.

"I take your point. Well, there's always Al Torstensson."

"He's not on the force anymore."

"No, he's chief of security for Boeing International. But he's got a lot of friends still on the force. Nobody will worry about them talking to him."

"Good point," Brognola said. "And we've got somebody from the Defense Intelligence Agency at Boeing. If he and Torstensson aren't working together, both of them ought to be fired."

"Al had his act together the last time we talked," Bolan said. "Is the FBI getting in on this, too?"

"If they say they want to, I can't stop them."

"They'll want to." Bolan disliked the prospect of tripping over FBI agents who didn't think his presidential pardon meant they had to cooperate with him. But he'd lived with it before.

He also had to admit that if he was in the FBI director's position, he'd certainly turn out every warm body he could get his hands on to find Corporal Goss. Right-wing terrorists sniffing around nuclear warheads weren't to be taken lightly.

"Afraid so," Brognola replied. "And don't forget the Marines. They've lost one of their own already. If they decide Goss is gone, we'll all be up to our midriffs in pissed-off jarheads."

That also made sense. Too much sense for Bolan's comfort, even though he sympathized with the Marines' attitude. This was a case with few clues so far, and if too many people got on the trail they'd trample everything flat.

"I'll get through to the DIA man and have him set things up with Torstensson," the big Fed said. "You can get your beauty sleep with a clear conscience."

Bolan's conscience wasn't completely clear. He knew that if he'd reached Seattle twenty-four hours earlier, Sam Brito might still be alive.

Now it was up to him to make sure the man's killer received his due.

2

Twilight was descending over Boeing International when Bolan climbed out of his rented van. After a bright morning the day had clouded. Now fog was creeping in again from the water.

Jet engines whined, roared, then split the dimness with tongues of orange-yellow flame. The flames revealed an AWACS on its takeoff run. Bolan watched the aircraft roll down the main runway. Suddenly the flames separated themselves from the earth, and a moment later the plane was banking to clear the mountains and head out to sea.

Bolan briefly wondered where it was headed. There weren't as many places that needed the big airborne radar jet now as there'd been a few years ago.

The twilight deepened as Bolan walked into the shadow of the isolated hangar. Here in a remote corner of the field, he was cut off from the runway lights and the spotlights around the main hangar and warehouses. A perfect place for a meeting—or an ambush.

From a small door in the weathered concrete wall to his right, the Executioner heard a whisper.

"Mike Belasko?"

The use of Bolan's cover name told him that security was good but not perfect.

"Uh-huh."

Bolan heard a safety click on. A moment later Al Torstensson loomed in the door.

"Hi, Mike. Long time no see."

"Long time too busy," the warrior replied. Torstensson punched the Executioner in the shoulder, and Bolan swayed back to ride the punch. The ex-cop was only a few years older than Bolan, bigger, broader and not at all out of shape.

They walked into the hangar. Torstensson had arranged the meet for the extreme rear of the two-hundred-foot-long building. Once the door was shut, they couldn't be taken from behind, and the hangar's main doors had long since frozen open. You could fly a jet through the front, but anybody coming in on the ground would show up like a fly on a plate.

As Torstensson locked the door, another man stepped out of the shadows. Bolan reached inside his windbreaker for the Beretta.

"Ellerbee, Defense Intelligence Agency."

The three men formed a shield around Torstensson's flashlight as Bolan examined Ellerbee's credentials. Finally he nodded.

"Okay, Ellerbee, you're on first. Why are we assuming the Silent Brotherhood is behind the hit on Brito?"

Ellerbee looked confused, then said, "The Silent Brotherhood is your standard right-wing white supremacist organization, with two differences. One of these differences is a fact, the other a rumor. The fact is that they've specifically targeted military personnel, particularly active-duty people in sensitive assignments.''

"Like Corporal Goss."

"Exactly. We have other examples, when you're cleared to have—"

Torstensson coughed and looked as if he wanted to get his hands around Ellerbee's neck. Bolan waved his friend to silence.

"Clearances won't be a problem. What's the rumor?"

"The rumor is that they're taking foreign money. Sources differ on where it's from—could be neo-Nazi, South African, Arab, even some of the anti-Semitic groups in Eastern Europe."

That made as much sense as anything anti-Semitic ever did. The United States was the home of the world's largest Jewish community and the principal protector of the second largest, Israel. Sabotage its armed forces, and the position of the Jews all over the world could become worse.

That wasn't Bolan's problem in believing Ellerbee on the Silent Brotherhood.

He still let the DIA man go on, until he was sure the man had run out of things to say, not just breath to say them. Bolan had his doubts about the DIA man, but doubts didn't always prove justified. Just most of the time.

"Okay," the warrior said. "The Silent Brotherhood isn't on anybody's nice-guy list. It certainly sounds like it'd be willing to waste anybody who pokes around the way Brito did. But do you guys know who Sam Brito's uncle is?"

"I do," Torstensson replied. "I even told Ellerbee here."

"Were you listening?" Bolan faced the DIA man. Even in the darkness the Executioner could see the man's sullen and defensive look.

"I didn't think a Mafia connection could be important here."

"Maybe it isn't," Bolan admitted. "Brito's never been part of Don Pietro's operations. The Families do have rules about not hitting that kind of relative. If they break those rules, there's usually a reason. Al, any ideas?"

Torstensson's expression said loudly that it was high time he got to talk about this to *somebody,* since Ellerbee wouldn't listen to him.

"Don Marco Capezzi is still numero uno around here," Torstensson told him. "You'd get an argument between the Britos and the Mangnanis about who's next. Zorino's definitely tail-end charlie.

"If the Families are in this, it'll be over Don Pietro's turf. He's old, and rumor has it that he's sick—heart trouble, I think. It could be one of the other Families moving in and trying to weaken Don Pietro with a hit on his favorite nephew."

"I thought you said the Families didn't go after, ah, noncombatants," Ellerbee said. He looked and sounded so out of his depth that Bolan almost felt sorry for him.

"Unless there's a good reason, I said," Bolan replied. "I'd guess Don Pietro Brito's turf is worth fifteen million tax-free dollars a year. For that kind of money a lot of people who aren't Mafia will break rules.''

"No shit," Ellerbee commented.

"Absolutely no shit," Torstensson said. "It could also be somebody inside the Britos with the same idea. In that case there's nothing we could do to the guy worse than what Don Pietro will do when he catches the SOB. The old Don still doesn't use turkey doctors, but Sam's killer will go out the hard way.''

"What about Brito deciding to join the Family business?" Ellerbee asked. "I've heard that he was short of money—''

The agent took a step backward as Torstensson glared at him.

"If you knew as much about Sam Brito as you were supposed to, you wouldn't have said that." Torstensson pushed his face close to Ellerbee's, making the man back away again.

"Okay. Okay. But this Mafia business leaves out one other possibility. Suppose there's a Silent Brotherhood connection with—''

Three shots rang out, fired just far enough apart that they could be counted.

Bolan's combat reflexes switched into high gear. He dived and rolled, taking Torstensson with him. The big security chief had already been in motion when Bolan helped him along.

Ellerbee was the only target, and even he was on the move when he took a bullet. A shot ripped into his thigh, spinning him half-around. Bolan and Torstensson jerked him the rest of the way around as they pulled him flat.

The Executioner had the Beretta drawn and was scanning the dark hangar when Torstensson whispered in his ear.

"Up there, on the catwalk above the door. I thought I saw something move."

Bolan looked up, and his keen night vision told him the same. Not much movement, but where there shouldn't be any at all...

"What's the layout of this place?" The warrior had memorized key features as he approached, but he needed details. Torstensson might know something that would save time or even lives.

"He can hit us before we reach the door you came in, or any of the other doors. At least if he's got an M-16, which is what it sounds like."

Bolan nodded. "Flash hider, but no night sight, or else he doesn't know how to use it. With a good night scope he should have nailed all three of us."

Torstensson grunted his agreement. Bolan knew that the man was thinking mostly of how to save them and take out their opponent, but his job meant asking a few other questions—such as how did the man get on the field? How did he get his *rifle* on the field? Was field security just sloppy, or had the men who sent the sniper bought off one of Torstensson's people?

"We can't get to the phone," the security chief added. "The nearest one's fifty feet away, all in the open. I'm getting on the radio to the main office. We've got what we don't call a SWAT team, but they do the same—"

"Dammit, no!" Ellerbee snarled. "You bring the cops in, and it blows my cover. If we take this guy out ourselves, I can hang in here. We can even pump him a bit."

"No way," Torstensson said. He spoke quietly but his tone was dangerous.

"There is a way. Mike—"

Two bullets slammed into the wall and one into the structural beam. As they ricocheted off concrete and metal, Ellerbee grabbed for the radio.

Torstensson tightened his grip on it with one hand and made a fist of the other. Ellerbee's hand clawed inside his jacket, but as it came out with a stainless-steel Colt Python, the Executioner's hand moved like a striking snake. It slammed Ellerbee's hand hard against the beam until his fingers opened and the Colt clattered to the floor.

"Ellerbee," Bolan said, "I can either take your gun away or I can let Al do what he was going to do. What's your choice?"

The agent rubbed his wrist and swore. Torstensson held the radio and after a moment he started to swear, too.

"Busted." He glared at the DIA man. "I dropped it when you went for that piece. If we don't get out of here because—"

"Hold it," the Executioner said in a commanding tone that silenced both men. "I've got to admit that Ellerbee's right. The less attention this gets, the better. I think it's worth trying to take that man without outside help. Al, when's your next check-in, and what's the response time if you don't make it?"

"Ten and ten."

So they had twenty minutes to deal with the sniper before Boeing's security team showed up. Even then, it might be only an ordinary car with a couple of men.

"You were saying about the layout . . . ?"

From Torstensson's description, Bolan saw one fairly good chance. Some of the supports for the catwalk that ran clear around the hangar were wide enough and thick enough to let him climb under cover. Once on the catwalk, there was a ladder to a roof hatch, and another hatch in the roof near the sniper's end of the building.

Even if Bolan didn't get farther than the catwalk, he'd have more mobility, enough to be a distraction to the sniper. He'd also be in a better position to warn security's first arrivals.

Warned, they wouldn't be any more welcome than before, but they also wouldn't be unsuspecting victims.

Bolan sketched his plan, and Torstensson nodded.

The Executioner fitted the stock and 20-round magazine to the 93-R. When he'd finished, he slapped his windbreaker. "There's a .44 Desert Eagle in here in case the sniper's friends show up in an armored car."

"Can I have my gun back?" Ellerbee asked.

Bolan glanced at Torstensson, and the security chief nodded reluctantly. Ellerbee gripped the Colt as if it would save him from drowning, and was checking the rounds as Bolan slipped away.

The warrior's first movements drew a burst from the sniper, at least ten rounds on full rock 'n' roll.

Bolan heard bullets ricocheting all over the place, but none of them hit anything.

He increased his speed. The sniper had shot off most of one magazine. If he shot off the rest and needed to change clips . . .

Bolan flung himself across the last open space before the structural support. The sniper tried to pick him off, one round close enough to clip the heel of his boot. Another seared a hot line across the small of his back.

Then Bolan was behind the cover provided by a latticework of rusty steel. He checked his watch. He had fourteen minutes left before security crashed this private party.

The sniper fired two bursts, then half a dozen aimed single rounds, as Bolan scrambled up the support. Some of them got through the latticework openings, but none reached Bolan. He heard ricochets, heard spent bullets clinking on the floor and thought he heard Al Torstensson cursing.

He didn't hear the sniper, and he wasn't going to stick his head beyond his handy protection to take a look.

The catwalk was forty feet above the floor. Bolan swung out from the support, shifted to a two-handed grip, then jackknifed up and over onto the catwalk itself. He pressed his face into rusty steel planking while more bullets whistled past him. He heard Torstensson curse.

Ten minutes to go, but security wasn't the only reason for speed now. If Torstensson was that angry, either he or Ellerbee could be in trouble. Bolan looked down the hangar.

He thought he saw someone crouched on the catwalk, well out of range for anything he was carrying, but not out of range for the M-16, and if the sniper had a reasonable supply of ammunition and a minimum amount of luck, he wasn't out of the fight yet.

The Executioner was sure he saw something the size and shape of a man about thirty feet to his left. Pulling himself along on his belly, barely breathing, the warrior covered fifteen of the thirty feet before he recognized the shape.

The object was a rolled-up tarpaulin, cracked and dusty, but just the right size to look like a man—in a dark hangar from two hundred feet away—to an opponent who might be getting a little desperate.

Bolan covered the last fifteen feet, grabbed the tarp and held it in front of him as he stood and balanced it on the railing. One hand gripped the rope around the canvas; the other drew the Beretta.

A triburst of 9 mm rounds flew toward the gunner, who replied with a salvo of 5.56 mm slugs. One sprayed rust chips into Bolan's eyes, another whistled past his cheek and four punched into the tarpaulin. Old and cracked as it was, the rolled canvas was thick enough to make an effective shield.

Bolan let out a yell of pain, heaved the tarp over the railing, then dropped to the catwalk floor. The sniper fired, as did Torstensson's big .44 Blackhawk.

The tarp thudded to the floor and sounded remarkably like a human body hitting the concrete. If it just looked and sounded the same to the sniper...

It did. The warrior saw a shadow detach itself from the far end of the hangar and slowly turn into a man— a man advancing with a rifle held over the railing, ready to cut down all opposition. The gunner obviously thought his opponents were down, but he wasn't going to count them out until he'd seen the bodies.

The man took on details—black sweater, black pants, black running shoes, a black ski mask over his face. His belt sagged under the weight of loaded magazines. He could keep the firefight going for quite a while if he wasn't taken out soon.

The Executioner shifted position, one muscle at a time, bringing the 93-R to bear. Another fifteen feet, and the man would be in extreme range for the Beretta. Another thirty, and he'd be dead.

The gunner covered only ten feet before Bolan saw him stiffen. The M-16 swung around, the muzzle probing the darkness. The warrior knew that the guy had spotted Torstensson and Ellerbee and was setting up for a killing burst.

Bolan had no choice despite the long range. He fired two tribursts.

The sniper's trigger finger tightened by sheer reflex, loosing a stream of 5.56 mm rounds that struck sparks from the oily concrete floor. The sniper straightened up as he fired, and Bolan got to his feet, the Beretta set for full-auto.

A string of rounds from the Beretta stitched the sniper from stomach to throat. He spun, lurched, but remained upright long enough to take two .44s from Torstensson's Blackhawk.

The man toppled over the railing and crashed forty feet to the concrete. He didn't move after he landed.

Bolan waited thirty seconds to be sure the man was dead and had no backup, then swung over the railing. In thirty seconds he'd rejoined Torstensson and Ellerbee.

The security chief was sitting by Ellerbee's head. The right sleeve of his blue shirt showed a wide bloody patch. Ellerbee lay still, and around his head was a pool of blood.

Bolan looked at Torstensson, who nodded. "Caught one of those ricochets in the neck. Bled out before I could do anything. Didn't make a sound, though."

Torstensson looked at his watch. "Okay, Mike. You've got four minutes—"

Sirens wailed in the distance.

"Make that *two* minutes to haul ass."

"Al, that arm—"

"Flesh wound at most. Maybe just a graze. I'll be shooting left-handed for a while. So haul ass, Mike. You're boss on this project. I'm boss here. And what the boss says is that the less time I have to spend explaining who you are and why you're here, the more I can do to squeeze old friends on the force. I'll have enough trouble explaining Ellerbee and what went down here."

The sirens were louder now. Torstensson lurched to his feet, waving off Bolan's assistance. "Just a little shocky. You're going to need somebody in the field with you, so I'll send you Monty Pelham. He's an ex-Air Police, and his last post was at SAC HQ in

Omaha. His real name's Grover, but don't call him that. He doesn't like it."

"Okay."

"I can still do a lot of phoning from a chair, so don't count me out. Now, like I was saying—get out of here!"

Bolan went out one end of the hangar just as security cars rolled up at the other end. By the time the hangar was surrounded, the Executioner was outside the illuminated area and jogging for the security fence circling the field.

3

Don Marco Capezzi sat behind a desk that resembled its owner. Both were large, dark, heavy, elderly, but still capable of much useful work.

In front of the desk stood Antonio Pescaglia, the Capezzi Family's chief hitter. He'd been standing there since entering the Don's office about three minutes ago. The Don was considering whether to let him sit, or make him stand for a minute or two more.

To be forced to stand before the Don's desk told you that he didn't approve of something you'd done. It didn't tell you what that something was or how much he disapproved.

During the thirty years he'd been the head of a Family, Don Marco had gained an evil reputation as a man who liked to see his enemies die hard. It was rumored that in his younger days he'd been an expert in handing out those hard deaths. It was no rumor that he liked to watch them.

"So. Our man at Boeing is dead, along with one of the men he was sent to kill. A pity about Torstensson. He was dangerous when he was a policeman. He might be dangerous again."

Capezzi saw Pescaglia begin to sweat. "Is there worse news that I haven't been told?"

"There is, but I only heard it myself on the way here, so I can only tell you what I heard."

"None of us is a mind reader, even Don Pietro Brito. I won't blame you for that. So what's the news?"

"Our man at the coroner's office telephoned me. He thinks there was a third man at the hangar. The sniper was killed by 9 mm bullets, but neither Torstensson nor the government man had 9 mm weapons."

"I see."

"There's more."

"Continue."

"The coroner is being asked by very powerful men not to mention this fact in his report. It appears that the federal government—or so I think—doesn't want the third man to be discovered."

"I agree." Capezzi motioned to a chair. "Sit down, my friend. Isn't that all?"

"I don't think so."

"What? You think the sniper might be identified?"

Pescaglia almost stood at the Don's tone of voice. Then he shook his head. "If he is identified, it will only be as a hanger-on of the Silent Brotherhood. We gave him some of their marked money. Even if he had lived, we were very careful to make him see us only as men of the Brotherhood."

"I should have expected such care from you, Antonio. Very well. So the dead sniper can't lead federal agents to us. Can anything lead us to the third man?"

"I think so. One of our men watching for the sniper's getaway saw a van drive off. Since it was foggy, our man took the chance of tailing the van."

"Yes?"

"It stopped at a house in Thomas. Unless I've been misinformed, I think it's a safehouse."

Don Marco agreed. He was certain that some Family operations had been seriously damaged by attacks coordinated by agents using the building as a base. He also knew that striking the house would draw the unwelcome attention of the authorities.

It would offend a Taiwanese who might now be a law-abiding citizen, but certainly had friends among the Tongs. Offending him meant offending the Tongs, and with a war among themselves drawing close, the Seattle Families had neither time nor men to spare for fighting on another front.

"Did he get a good look at the man?"

"Tall, dark, athletic, wearing a black windbreaker. He drew a gun as he approached the house, and it looked like a Beretta with a shoulder stock."

Capezzi stiffened. The description sounded chillingly familiar. But if it *was* who he thought it was, surely the man had detected the tail?

Probably, but not certainly. The man in question was good, perhaps the best there was. He wasn't so perfect that he might not miss someone trailing him on a foggy night.

The Don reached into a drawer of his desk and pulled out a bottle of homemade wine. "There are glasses in the china cabinet by the door, Antonio." He pushed the bottle across the desk.

"Thank you, Don Marco."

"And I thank you, and the man who did the tailing. He might have put us in a position to add a million dollars to our coffers."

"A million? Then the man may be—"

"Exactly. Reward the man who did the tailing. Also send out a description of our friend. Anywhere he appears, asking about the Silent Brotherhood, I want to know of it at once."

"That could put some of our informants in danger, with all due respect, Don Marco."

"If we don't ready ourselves for battle against the Executioner, we are *all* in danger."

THE GRAY WATER LAPPED at the stony beach, tossing forth driftwood and pulling it back like a playful cat with a mouse. A mile offshore a Trident missile submarine was plowing her way north.

Between the submarine and the shore, a small boat bobbed, with men tending lines stretched over the side. Even without the eagle, globe and anchor on the bow, Bolan would have recognized Marines in fatigues.

The Marine gunnery sergeant beside the Executioner wasn't in the mood to answer questions about Major Brito and Corporal Goss.

Bolan didn't blame the man, but the questions had to be asked, and the less officially, the better. Gunny Cullom didn't have to answer them, but the more he answered, the better. At the moment he was the only man around who'd really known both Brito and Goss well.

"Okay," Cullom said. "If it's to the point where they're dragging for Goss's body—" he jerked a thumb toward the boat "—I guess it's serious. But tell me why I should talk to *you*."

The warrior had already mentioned his credentials, and Cullom had told him what to do with them.

"I can do more than most to bring in the people who killed Brito."

"What about Goss?"

"I didn't think you cared so much—"

For a moment Bolan thought Cullom was going to swing at him. Then the gunny laughed.

"Walked right into that one, didn't I? Okay. But tell me, why should I believe you'll do better than the police?"

"I have contacts that they don't."

"And I'm supposed to take your word for it?"

"Either that, or do everything through channels."

"No way," Cullom said. "Last time they came through on one of my problem kids, they kept trying to make out he was a fairy. They never thought of asking his girlfriends."

"Was Goss a problem?"

"In nine years and only a corporal? He had problems, I'd say. But he wasn't one. Maybe that's why nobody took a hand with him until it was too late."

Bolan recognized the note of self-blame in Cullom's voice. A good NCO, he suspected that Goss's disappearance might be partly his fault. The warrior remained silent.

Cullom didn't need much more prompting. Goss had been a loner who did everything you told him to do perfectly but never anything more.

"If we hadn't been short of cadre, I doubt he'd have ever made corporal. But that was the gunny before me. Can't pull somebody's stripes just because you don't agree with the guy before you."

"No." In his time Bolan had seen men fragged for doing that—officers, not just NCOs.

"Wasn't a discipline problem, either. No drugs, no booze, no chasing women. Just got off by himself and read stuff."

"What kind of stuff? I've heard he bad-mouthed some of the black Marines."

"Who told you that?"

"I'm not sure I can tell you."

"Can't, or won't?"

Bolan was silent.

Cullom glared. "Look. They can't court-martial me for not washing the Corps' dirty linen in public. Get that through your head."

"My head's in fine shape," Bolan said sharply. "It's Goss's and Sam Brito's heads we need to worry about."

Cullom's shoulders slumped. "I guess you're right. Okay. Goss bad-mouthed anybody who tried to break through that shell. Didn't matter if they were black, white, brown, pink or purple with green polka dots. He'd tell them to go to hell, and not be too nice about it."

That wasn't the way Bolan had heard it, but he'd expect Cullom to defend one of his men. Also it was possible that the sergeant was right and what Bolan had heard was wrong.

Goss and the Silent Brotherhood? If the leaders of the organization had heard only the rumors, they might have thought Goss would go for their brand of armed bigotry. When they approached him, they might have looked good to a lonely, unhappy young man. Someplace where he could belong.

Then they could have started asking for things he didn't want to give. Desperate, Goss turned to Brito. The Silent Brotherhood struck, taking out Brito and kidnapping Goss. The corporal was probably dead meat by now, too.

The Silent Brotherhood might be involved after all. It was a coincidence that they'd pulled this off right about the time Brito's uncle was facing a Mafia war. But something being a coincidence didn't make it impossible.

"All right," Bolan said. "I think you've helped a lot. But if you remember something, or something comes up you don't want to send through channels..."

He handed Cullom a card. "Memorize that number. If you call it, ask for Mike Belasko. I won't be there most of the time, but somebody reliable will. I'll get in touch."

"Can do."

Cullom left first. Bolan let him get a hundred yards away before cutting back cross-country toward the facility's guest parking lot.

A flight of antisubmarine Vikings whistled overhead as the Executioner approached the van. He scanned the immediate area, then studied the doors for any sign of tampering.

Normally when on a mission he changed vehicles as often as every forty-eight hours. This time he'd kept the van into a third day.

Keeping the van could be dangerous, like painting a big bull's-eye on his chest. But it might also draw the enemy into the open, tempted by the chance of taking him out.

He climbed into the van and made another check for tampering. Still nothing. As the warrior keyed the ignition, a silver-gray Buick stopped directly in front of the vehicle, blocking Bolan's exit.

His hand darted inside his jacket as the Buick's windows rolled down. Two Ingram subguns stared at Bolan through the windshield. He started to fling himself to the right, across the seat, out the passenger door and into action.

Then he glanced in the rearview mirror. A woman in yellow slacks was shepherding three children into a station wagon. The youngest child, a girl about four, was clutching a teddy bear in a naval aviator's costume.

Bolan had a good chance of taking out the hardmen in the Buick. He had no chance at all of taking them out before those Ingrams got off a burst. With bullets literally flying all over the lot, the children and their mother would be lucky to escape uninjured.

So would anybody else in the line of fire, which meant quite a lot of territory when two Ingrams on full automatic were in the hands of hardmen who didn't much care about innocent bystanders.

The Executioner straightened, holding his hands away from his body. He rested them on the top of the steering wheel for a moment, then pointed at the driver's door. One of the hardmen nodded.

Bolan climbed out, to find not only two Ingrams but also an Uzi pointed at him.

"Thanks for making it easy," the man with the Uzi said. All three men had the same look about them—men who lived by the gun and by the fear, money and blood of innocent victims.

"I needed a vacation anyway." One of the gunners took his Beretta and ushered him into the back seat of the Buick.

4

The Buick drove up hills and down through valleys for what Bolan guessed was about half an hour. Several times they passed police cars, but the hitters knew how to handle that. One kept a muzzle jabbed into Bolan's ribs. A second kept his weapon trained on the police. A third would stay alert, ready to take out any witnesses.

The ride went on beyond half an hour, but now the car traveled on more-level ground. Bolan didn't care to risk moving his head to either side, but through the windshield he could see that they were in farming country. They soon left the main roads, then paved ones, and finally rolled onto a dirt track through an apple orchard.

The Executioner could smell the sea, which told him very little. Pretending to ease stiff neck muscles, he twisted his head a few degrees to the right.

The cold hard metal of an Ingram jabbed into his neck. Bolan straightened his head again. As he did, something sharp slid through his clothing into the flesh of his thigh.

A moment later his head began to sink onto his chest. It seemed to weigh a ton, and when he tried to lift it his neck muscles screamed in protest. Then his neck muscles stopped obeying his will. His eyelids did the same. They drifted shut, leaving him in darkness.

BOLAN AWOKE STRIPPED to his underwear and lying on a filthy, musty mattress. Other than a bucket that stood in for a toilet, the mattress was the only furniture in the room.

The room itself was about eight feet square and higher than it was wide. The walls were peeling paint, and the floors were wide pine planks, as dirty as the mattress and liberally covered with mouse droppings.

Comfort Bolan did not have, although to be sure he hadn't expected it. Light he had in plenty. A bare two-hundred-watt bulb blazed down from a cord in the ceiling, and a dusty window of Victorian leaded glass let in more light from outside.

Bolan saw that the window wasn't barred and walked over to investigate. The land gave way to a hundred-foot drop to jagged rocks with surf boiling over them. Even if he made it through the window and jumped as far outward as he could, he'd never reach water deep enough to break his fall.

Escape through the window meant only suicide. Bolan had always accepted the idea of someday not getting out of a situation alive. He'd never accepted the idea of going without taking as many of the predators with him as he could.

Whatever drug they'd used had left him thirsty and hung over, with muscle aches in unaccustomed places. He could do nothing about the thirst, but deep breathing drove away some of the headache. It also began to unkink the muscles, and a series of exercises finished that job.

Bolan had finished his exercises when the door slid open. Three men entered, one carrying a small briefcase, as well as a revolver in a shoulder holster. The other men carried an Ingram and a Star 9 mm pistol respectively. They positioned themselves so that they could take out Bolan without getting caught in the cross fire.

This alertness told the warrior that now wasn't the time to make his move.

As the man with the briefcase pulled out a hypodermic syringe, Bolan covertly studied him. His face showed the signs of recent scarring—skin grafts for a burn or plastic surgery for a disguise? Take away the skin grafts and go by height, build and facial bone structure—the man could be Louis Garrado.

Louis and Frank Garrado had been the only brother turkey doctors in the underworld, until the day Frank was found dead in a Seattle back-alley trash bin—not only dead, but tortured the same way he'd tortured so many victims until death for them was a merciful release from hell.

Now Louis was working solo, unless the rumors that he'd set up with the Capezzi Family were to be believed. Bolan believed them. Don Marco still liked the sight of blood. He didn't have much time to shed it personally, so it would make sense for him to hire an expert. Louis Garrado was certainly that.

The needle slammed into Bolan's arm. It bit deep, but into muscle rather than into a vein. Only small blood vessels lay in its path to spread the drug through

Bolan's system. The muscles themselves would absorb most of it.

The Executioner breathed shallowly as the needle jerked around in his flesh. Garrado was obviously trying to start the pain right now. In fact, he might be more interested in the pain than in how much of the drug was going into his victim.

Bolan twisted his face into a mask of agony, doing his best to imitate a man hurting badly but trying to keep quiet.

He had proof the trick had worked a moment later, when Garrado jerked the needle free. The man was smiling, almost grinning. The two hardmen were looking suspiciously at Bolan, as if the Executioner had to be tougher than that.

They also held their guns just a trifle more loosely than previously.

As the door slid shut behind the departing men, Bolan lay down and pretended to go under. His slow, regular breathing would have convinced any unseen watcher that the drug had hit him.

Two minutes later he knew that his gamble had paid off. He'd absorbed only a fraction of the intended dose of the drug. Now all he needed to do was to make sure that anyone watching him saw what they expected—the Executioner, drugged and helpless.

The egotistical Garrado certainly wouldn't admit that he might have been tricked. The two hardmen might even be wondering if the man on the mattress *was* the Executioner.

The next visitors might not be so alert, and against Mack Bolan, anything less than complete alertness was fatal. There were plenty of men who could testify to that—if you could hear the evidence of ghosts.

BOLAN PRETENDED to be asleep for what he guessed to be about an hour. During that time he heard sea-birds, the surf, a foghorn and the answering foghorn of a passing ship. He thought he heard a boat's motor, probably a low-speed diesel.

None of these told him anything except that he was close to navigable water.

The house looked old and had to be in a fairly isolated spot to keep people from asking questions about what went on inside. On the coast and up toward the mouth of the sound were plenty of old houses built by long-dead lumber barons. Some lay just close enough to civilization to attract renovators. Others might as well have been in Tahiti.

Bolan suspected that he'd be on his own even if he managed to escape. There'd be no police and no neighbors to help. There'd also be a chase, by men who'd gone to considerable trouble to capture the Executioner in the first place. They'd be anxious to run him down before he reached safety and exposed their stronghold.

He decided to get a couple of hours of genuine sleep. The risk of his captors taking him while he slept was real enough. So was the certainty that he'd need all his strength when they did come.

The position he'd assumed wasn't the most comfortable for sleeping, but he managed to doze for a while before he heard footsteps outside the door.

It sounded like considerably more than three men, and Bolan was instantly alert. He forced himself to lie still, even limp, as the door slid open.

The same two hardmen who'd been there earlier entered the room, one carrying a pair of handcuffs. Garrado was nowhere in sight.

The hardman with the cuffs kicked Bolan over onto his stomach, then snapped on the cuffs. The warrior mentally noted that his "drugged" act was still working. The second hardman wasn't keeping his Ingram so carefully pointed at the prisoner this time.

Even more important, the chain connecting the cuffs was just a little too long. A strong, limber man like Bolan could almost certainly bring his hands up over his head. Then he could make a fight of it, a good one if he got hold of a gun and a decent one even if he didn't.

Both hardmen now dragged Bolan roughly to his feet. He mumbled and grunted incoherently.

A square, balding man appeared in the doorway, toting a Smith & Wesson 25-5. Bolan recognized the face—Antonio Pescaglia had been a known hit man for the Families for more than twenty years, and the top hitter for the Capezzis for at least ten. He was also even more bloodthirsty than the average member of his profession.

He and Don Marco, Bolan knew, were well matched.

"Easy, you clowns!" Pescaglia snapped. "Garrado's almost ready for him. Don't think he won't notice if you put your friend back under."

Bolan saw one hardman actually turn pale at the implied threat. Then the warrior let his head bob limply to look at the other.

As he did, a scream floated up from what seemed an unimaginable distance below. It was the scream of someone who'd thought there was nothing worse than hell and now had learned differently. Bolan couldn't tell whether it was a man or a woman, the voice was so twisted by pain.

He pretended to flinch. They'd probably let him hear the scream as a bit of psychological warfare. Knowing what was going on downstairs might soften him up—not that this would stop Garrado, a man who loved his work.

The hardmen jerked Bolan forward through the doorway. Pescaglia stepped back, and several other men made room for him.

One of them was a tall young man with blond hair in a military crew cut, a man with a string of hot-air balloons tattooed on his right forearm—a man the Executioner hadn't expected to see alive and certainly not here.

Corporal Richard Goss of the United States Marine Corps.

5

If Mack Bolan had ever let surprise slow him, he'd have been dead years ago. He'd taken bigger surprises than Goss without blinking.

So he took half a second to study the Marine. He was unbound but unarmed, looked healthy and un-afraid, but seemed to be uneasy in his present company. What this added up to, Bolan would consider later.

In the next half second the Executioner realized that the men in the hall had slipped into a vulnerable for-mation. Too many of them were too close to him for safety, and too close to one another to let their friends shoot freely.

They were also between him and every door except one, which seemed to lead to the basement. That also was something to worry about later, if there was a later.

In the next half second Bolan moved.

He flung himself sideways, slamming one hardman into the wall. At the same time the warrior lashed to the right with his free foot. Driven by a muscular leg and flawless timing, the foot smashed into the hardman's groin. The man's scream echoed through the hall and froze everyone but his tormentor.

That freeze lasted long enough for Bolan, too long for everybody else. The Executioner followed through on the kick and sideslip, going into a roll, arms up over his head. Muscles screamed and joints howled, but he came up with his hands in front of him.

He also came up facing the basement door, just as Louis Garrado stepped through it. Garrado had a Browning Hi-Power in his hand, but not the reflexes to use it. For too many years he'd done his work with tools other than guns, on people in no position to resist.

Bolan's hands slammed upward, knocking the Browning to the floor. They continued their upward trajectory into Garrado's larynx, the man's cartilage shattering under the impact. Garrado reeled, clawing at his throat. For good measure Bolan slammed him against the edge of the doorway, hard enough for the torturer to crack his skull against the tough wood.

The other Capezzi gunners had been holding their fire while Garrado and Bolan faced off. By the time they realized that their invaluable turkey doctor was dying on his feet, Bolan was on his way down the basement stairs.

The Executioner took just long enough to throw the bolt behind him, then leaped down the stairs three at a time. At the bottom was another door; he heaved that shut, dropped the bar in place, then pushed every heavy object he could reach against the door.

Bolan had made it hard for himself to get out, but even harder for the Capezzis to get in. If he'd had a chance to take out Pescaglia, he'd have said the odds were in his favor.

With Pescaglia still alive, the odds were about even. But Garrado's death was a fair-sized victory all by itself. It would save a good many people a lot of pain.

It might even force Don Marco Capezzi into the open to do his own dirty work on prisoners. Then he'd be easier prey.

That was as much strategic analysis as Bolan needed. The rest of his job now was solving a tactical problem: getting out of the place alive, with as many Capezzi Family soldiers dead as possible.

His first step was to explore the basement. A quick look around suggested that it had only one interior entrance. A flashlight hanging beside the lower door confirmed this. It also suggested that half the basement had been renovated, half left as a junk room. It looked as if everything the past few owners hadn't needed had been carried down the stairs.

One of the items left behind was an old rusty file. It took Bolan longer than he liked to file through the handcuff chains, but he had both hands free within minutes. He also had a length of chain dangling from each wrist, which he knew could be a vicious weapon in a close-quarters fight.

Garrado wasn't a hired gun, but at least he kept his weapon oiled and loaded. Bolan satisfied himself that he had a working Hi-Power with a full 13-round magazine. He also satisfied himself that the noises upstairs didn't mean an immediate assault on the basement stairs.

He began a tour of the basement, noting every-thing in the piles of discards that could cut, burn, ex-plode or crush. Improvising weapons was something the Special Forces had raised to a fine art, and Bolan had been a good artist even by Special Forces stan-dards. He'd sharpened his skills still further in the fighting he'd done afterward, in a blacksuit instead of fatigues.

He'd begun to wonder why the whole house hadn't caught fire from spontaneous combustion in the basement rubbish piles, when he heard a moan. At least it sounded like a moan, and from a living throat.

With the Browning in one hand and a crowbar in the other, he headed toward the source of the noise, which seemed to come from behind a padlocked door that led to the renovated part of the basement. The crow-bar made quick work of the hasp, and Bolan stepped through a low doorway into hell.

He stopped cataloging the instruments of torture when he reached the blowtorch. Nothing had sur-prised him. He knew what else he'd probably find as he heard the groan again.

This time he traced it to its source, in a small side room just large enough to hold a blood-spattered mattress. On the mattress lay what had been a human being. At first Bolan couldn't even tell whether it was a man or a woman. Then a closer look revealed why he couldn't tell.

The man had also lost one eye, and the other was half-closed from bruises and dried blood. But he managed to focus it on Bolan. He couldn't speak, but the eye was eloquent enough in its pleading for mercy.

The shot echoed around the torture chamber, but silence followed, both downstairs and upstairs. After a moment Bolan heard someone muttering, "Maybe the bastard shot himself," and an obscene reply from Pescaglia.

Pescaglia might know who he had downstairs. He certainly knew about not underestimating an opponent. Bolan picked up the blowtorch and an armful of other items he expected to find useful and left Garrado's torture chamber.

He knew now that the house seemed to be built into the side of a hill. All the windows and the basement door to the hillside were on the downhill side. The two windows in the torture chamber were boarded up, and it would take too long to rip out the boards.

The two windows and door in the other half of the basement were still useable. Bolan peered through the filthy glass of the right-hand window and saw rain-slick grass and masses of shrubbery. The grass was a foot high, and the shrubbery hadn't been pruned in years. If he could get out of the basement, he'd have good concealment for quite a distance.

A blast of blazing light suddenly struck Bolan like a physical blow. When his vision cleared, he saw that floodlights from overhead and in the shrubbery were lighting up the lawn. A cat couldn't have made it through the grass without being spotted.

And what was spotted out there would die. Bolan counted at least four men, all with automatic weapons or at least rifles. Numbers, firepower and range would all be against him.

But outside he'd at least have a chance. Inside he could only wait to die like a rat in a trap. He wouldn't give the men he'd fought so long that easy a victory.

Bolan quickly began pulling his arsenal together. One of Garrado's instruments had started life as a glass cutter. With it, the warrior carefully cut nearly all the way around the two windows. He also sawed nearly all the way through the lock on the cellar door. Now he could snap the metal with a thumb and fore-finger.

Then he began collecting oily rags, old bedding and anything else that would burn. He made four piles, each bound with half-rotted twine. One lay in front of each window and the outside door. The last he set down in front of the door to the main floor.

The noise from upstairs was now entirely footsteps and not so many of those. Pescaglia was obviously redeploying his troops. He must have also reminded them that it wasn't a good idea to discuss plans where the enemy might overhear! If Bolan could finish off Pescaglia, as well as Garrado, tonight, he'd blow a hole in the Capezzi Family that Don Marco might never fill.

No point in waiting any longer to take the fight to the enemy. Bolan tested the blowtorch, saw that its gas tank was nearly full, and touched the flame to the first bundle. He'd already moved the trunks and old anvils clear of the inside door. Now all he needed was to flip up the bar, jerk the door open and toss the flaming, smoke-belching bundle into the stairway.

As he barred the door again, he heard angry shouts from upstairs. The wood of the old house had to be tinder dry. The fire on the stairs should at least have everybody in the house thinking of their backs. It might even drive them pell-mell into the open, giving Bolan more targets.

Now for the other exits. One window out, with a tinkle of shattering glass that drew a blast of slugs. Another Uzi, Bolan decided. The 9 mm tumblers chipped stone and splintered wood, stinging his face, but didn't keep him from tossing the second bundle out.

The second window went faster and drew no attention. As Bolan started to open the outside door, he heard footsteps directly overhead, and Pescaglia's voice. It sounded as if the rest of the Capezzi soldiers were leaving the house to join the watch in the shrubbery.

Bolan frowned. He'd hoped they'd do that at the last minute and carelessly. If Pescaglia was keeping his men under such good control...

The Executioner set the thought aside. He'd lived with the knowledge that one day he'd reach the end of the road, facing odds too long for any man. If he died tonight, it would be with a good deal of company from the Capezzi Family.

The bar to the outside door slid aside. Smoke billowed as Bolan touched off the last and largest bundle. It was becoming difficult to breathe in the basement, as smoke seeped through the two windows and the other door. But the smoke would make him a harder target.

A heavy automatic weapon rattled from far downhill. In the moment before shouts drowned it out, Bolan recognized an H&K G-3 assault rifle. Then the 7.62 mm slugs from the rifle chewed their way across the front of the house. The daylight on the lawn turned to twilight as the overhead floodlights died.

Bolan launched himself through the door, slamming the ancient wood aside with head and shoulders, leaping into the open like a missile. He landed in a roll, coming up with the Browning ready to fire as the unknown rifleman opened up again.

This time the man shot out one of the floodlights on the lawn. The hardmen in the bushes turned their attention and their weapons downhill. Bursts of automatic gunfire flailed away at the dark trees.

Bolan rose enough to sight on the last floodlight and take it out with a shot at near-maximum range. As darkness swallowed the lawn, more 7.62 mm slugs chopped into the front of the house.

A gunner who'd come out of the building let out a yell of surprise and pain. Several of his comrades opened fire, sending bullets well clear of Bolan but not so clear of their comrades in the bushes.

Bolan smiled grimly as he heard Pescaglia screaming obscenities at the men by the house. More obscenities flew back from the bushes. In the confusion both sides stopped firing, and in the darkness the Executioner was through the bushes before anyone noticed.

By the time he could turn and look back at the house, it was burning. The fire on the inside stairs had reached the ground floor, and smoke was rolling out of half the ground-floor windows. Flames were also climbing up the outside of the house, feeding on ancient dry wood. It was a splendid old Victorian place that must have stood a hundred years. It would be ashes by morning.

The burning house would force the Capezzis into the open. If Bolan could just find a place where he could cut off their retreat, he could reverse the whole course of tonight's fight. If the unknown rifleman stayed on his side, he might break Don Marco's Family here and now.

Bolan began to stalk the men scattered through the bushes. He needed another weapon. As long as his enemies were too busy keeping their heads down to watch their flanks or rears, they were the best source to provide one.

The Executioner caught his first man beside a stand of forsythia. A thrown pebble drew the man's attention, and a sudden rush brought Bolan into striking range. The crowbar descended like the wrath of God, and the hardman was taken out of play.

Bolan pressed on, now armed with a .45 Ingram with three magazines.

The rifleman was still in action. Every time Pescaglia tried to lead his men away from the house, bullets stitched a dead line in their path. It was as if the rifleman had no quarrel with them as long as they stayed out of the fight.

Suddenly one of the house's turrets spewed flame. It then tottered, swung outward and crashed to the ground. It missed the crouching hardmen by mere feet, and snapped Pescaglia's control over them.

Like one man, they dashed downhill. Pescaglia screamed curses after them, then flames boomed through the wall just above his head. Brushing cinders from his hair, he sprinted after his men.

The rifleman didn't fire a shot. Bolan squeezed off two bursts from the Ingram, hitting two men. Both went down but neither was Pescaglia.

The running men, though, decided that their comrades in the bushes were shooting at them. They went to ground, crawled to whatever concealment they could find and returned fire. A nice little firefight built up, with the two bands of Capezzi hardmen blazing away at each other as fast as they could.

Bolan would have laughed if he hadn't been too busy trying to take advantage of this confusion. All the men downhill were now looking to their front, and if he could close in before Pescaglia got his men in line—

Bullets flew over Bolan's head, chopping twigs and leaves from a tree and spraying bark into his face. He recognized the G-3. He also recognized that he'd come within six inches of being blown away.

As Bolan hit the dirt, he heard a voice calling.

"Belasko, are you okay?"

It was a voice pitched just loud enough to carry over the roar of the flames and the occasional shot. It was also oddly high-pitched if it was a man's voice, but it didn't sound like a woman's.

"Belasko. How about an answer?"

It could be a ruse to force him to reveal his position, but it could also be a friendly gesture.

"Belasko okay," he called.

The reply reached some of the Capezzis. With more optimism than judgment, they blazed away into the darkness. None of the bullets closed in on Bolan.

The rifleman promptly opened up again, this time at the hardmen, shooting to kill. The scream and thrashing effectively silenced the man's comrades. In the silence Bolan heard the high-pitched voice again.

"Belasko, we've done enough for tonight."

"I haven't."

"Then you've got to do the rest without my help. Do you think that's wise?"

Bolan studied the hillside and the Capezzi positions revealed by the blazing fire. The opposition still had at least a dozen able-bodied men, and he had only two guns with limited ammunition. With Pescaglia getting his men in order, Bolan's chances of getting more ammo would be slim. The mafioso's chances of overwhelming the Executioner by sheer weight of numbers would be good.

Tonight's fight had cost the Capezzis five or six men. That wasn't enough to destroy them, but it was enough to hurt. The rifleman was making sense.

"Rifleman, thanks for the advice. I'll take it."

"Good. How much of a head start do you want?"

Bolan wished he knew more of the ground beyond the trees. "Where are their cars?"

"They've got two vans and a Cadillac at the bottom of the hill. They had a Blazer in the garage, but it's only a blaze now."

"Ten minutes." That would let Bolan disable the other three vehicles. On foot he was confident he

could stay ahead of any number of city-bred hardmen.

"You've got it. My word of honor on it. And Belasko..."

"Yes?"

"Thanks for disposing of Garrado. We don't need
people like him."

That, Bolan thought as he headed off into the
darkness, was the understatement of the year.

6

The moist warm air of the greenhouse was heavy with the smell of growing plants. The first tomatoes were already appearing on the vines.

Don Pietro Brito looked at the two men standing in front of his lounge chair for a moment longer. Then he motioned them to be seated.

The man born Leon Fieromosca but called "the Shadow" sat down as gracefully as he did everything else. The *consigliere* wasn't as graceful, but then he was nearly as old as Don Pietro. Arthritis was doing to him what an ailing heart had already nearly done to the Don.

"So, Shadow. Tell me again of the battle at the Capezzi safehouse, which you and the other man made so unsafe. I would like to hear a good story again, and my old friend here hasn't heard it at all."

The Shadow spoke quickly but quietly, in that high-pitched voice that made some doubt his manhood. *Had* made some doubt it, before he proved to the women that he had manhood in plenty and to the men that they should keep their mouths shut.

"Then the Capezzis have lost at least six men, including Garrado," the Don concluded, when the Shadow was finished.

"Not less than that. I was careful not to kill the man I wounded in front of the house, or the man I interrogated. Having no drugs, I had to be quick and harsh in the interrogation. I know this is against your—"

Don Pietro dismissed the apology. "I know you aren't an animal like the Garrados, nor will you turn into one overnight. Be easy in your mind about that, and let us pass on to other matters."

Cautiously Don Pietro sat up. His doctors had cursed him with an order to do everything cautiously.

"Is this man the one we seek?"

The Shadow shrugged. "If he isn't the same man, then he's one equally able to do what we wish of him. Indeed, it might be as well if he was somebody else. There's a million-dollar price on the head of only one man. Also, the Commission in New York—"

"Bah," Don Pietro said, sounding as if he wanted to spit. "Those old men sitting and dreaming of the days when they carried guns will not hear of what I plan until I've done it. Even then, they'll also hear that I did it to prevent a war among the Seattle Families. They know what that can lead to."

"I think the Don has the right of it," the *consigliere* said politely. "I also think it's bad luck to wish that there be two men like the Executioner. One of him has done enough damage over the years."

"There is that, too," the Shadow said, more politely than sincerely. "Very well, I'll continue to the next step of the plan."

BOLAN WAS STEPPING out of the shower when the telephone rang. He thought it might be Monty Pelham, phoning to say that he'd been delayed. He decided to finish drying off and let the answering machine take the call.

The caller wasn't Monty Pelham. It was the same voice he'd heard on the hill the previous night.

"Mr. Belasko, it's the man with the G-3 who helped you out last night. I'd like to talk to you again, without people shooting at us. If you call me at this number, we can arrange something." The voice repeated a number and an extension twice, said goodbye and hung up.

Bolan's first call wasn't to the mystery man; it was to Hal Brognola.

The big Fed listened to the recording of the call in silence. "That's not much for a voice-print analysis," he said finally.

"No, but it's a start. This is the first lead we have on the rifleman's identity. I owe him."

"Okay, okay. I'll give it to Aaron. Has Pelham called yet?"

"No."

"If it won't be poaching on your range, Striker, I'd like to put a fire under his tail."

Bolan didn't bother asking why. Brognola had spent more years than he had in fighting the predators, even if he'd always done it within the limits of the law. He had most of Bolan's instincts for telling when a situation might become deadly at a moment's notice or none at all.

"Go ahead. I'll call you back as soon as I contact our rifleman."

BOLAN CALLED THE NUMBER three times without reaching the man he wanted. Monty Pelham showed up just after the third call, matching Torstensson's description and giving the right recognition code. He also carried himself with the best kind of self-confidence—that of a man who's so sure he's good that he doesn't have to prove it.

They were talking cautiously about mutual friends in the security field when the telephone rang.

"Mr. Belasko. I'm sorry I was out when you called. Are you alone?"

"Yes."

"Good." The voice adopted a more formal diction. "I can speak in the name of Don Pietro Brito. He wishes to meet with you to discuss matters of mutual interest and profit."

"What sort of matters?"

"I'd tell you if Don Pietro had told me."

"Then either he doesn't trust you or he can't make up his mind how badly he wants to talk to me. Either way, is it worth my while to come and be jerked around—or worse?"

The voice sounded genuinely insulted. "If you know Don Pietro's reputation, you'll know that no one has ever been harmed while a guest under his roof.

"I can say this—he and you have enemies in common, and it will do you no harm to listen to him tell you who they are."

"That might be so," Bolan agreed. He knew it might have been wise to apologize for doubting Don Pietro's honor, but he couldn't say the words. The "honor" of mafiosi was not even a bad joke with the Executioner.

"It is so," the voice said. "You may think what you wish about the Families' honor. However, if you don't wish to call Don Pietro honorable, can you at least call him wise? When he knows that he can't fight everyone at once?"

"I'll buy that." It matched what the Executioner knew about the reclusive and shrewd head of the Brito Family.

"Good. Then may I offer you advice on how best to meet Don Pietro?"

"If I don't have to promise to take it."

"No obligation, as the salesmen say."

The "advice" was detailed directions for a meeting with the speaker, who would pick up Bolan and take him to the meeting with the Don. If "Mike Belasko" needed to inform someone of his intentions, that was acceptable, as long as the person was discreet.

"You are truly in no danger from us. But I beg you to believe me that we might all be in danger if the persons you informed were indiscreet. Indeed, they might also be in danger—and very horrible danger, too. A certain Family hasn't lost its gift for torture merely because the Garrados are dead."

"I've heard as much," Bolan said shortly. "All right. I'll call you back in—" he looked at his watch "—two hours. And *be* there when I call, or no deal."

"As you wish."

Bolan hung up and played back the recording for Pelham.

"If they were handing out prizes for stone-ground weirdness, that cat'd be in the finals," Pelham commented.

"No argument there," Bolan said as he dialed Brognola's number.

IT WAS TEN MINUTES SHORT of the two hours when Brognola rang back.

"We've got an ID on the voice."

"Do I have to wait for it? I'm supposed to call back in ten minutes or no deal."

"I don't know if you'll want to call back. It's Leon Fieromosca."

"The Britos' top hitter?"

"Ninety-six and a butt percent certain."

"As our mutual friend Mr. Pelham said, this is beginning to take some sort of prize for weirdness."

"Ain't that the truth."

"What sort of reputation does Fieromosca have?"

"Meaning, can he make an offer without the Don's knowledge and consent? Or can he keep the other hitters off you for the length of the meeting?"

"Both."

The silence was longer than Bolan usually had from Brognola. Finally the big Fed sighed.

"Given that it's not my ass on the line—"

"Hal, you don't need to reassure me that you value mine as much as you do your own. We're wasting time."

"Okay. In something this important, Fieromosca wouldn't have picked up the phone unless he had Don Pietro's okay. He also can keep the other hitters away long enough for the meeting. If it's short enough, they may not even learn about it. Even if they do, they'll think twice before trying to collect the bounty on your head. They know they'd never live to spend money earned by taking out one of Don Pietro's guests."

That made just enough sense. On the principle of "know thy enemy," Bolan had a mental file of the Mafia's best soldiers, and Fieromosca was high up toward the top. He'd earned his war name of the Shadow by his silent and unstoppable kills.

"All right. I'm going to lay a few conditions on the Shadow. If he accepts them without consulting with Don Pietro, I'll make the meeting."

Bolan hung up and looked at Pelham.

"Did Torstensson tell you exactly what you're getting into?"

Pelham shrugged. "The chief's the chief. I don't sweat the little details when he asks a favor."

"You might be asked to do things that will be outside the law. I have—connections—that might keep me clean, no matter what. They probably wouldn't stretch to cover you."

"I'll take that chance. Worst they can do is shoot me, and why'd I put on a uniform if that bugged me?"

"That's not the worst," Bolan went on. "Worse could happen to you. Worse could happen to your family, and I've heard you've got a wife and two kids."

"Wife dumped me a couple years back. My mom's got the kids. They're growing up okay, so far."

"If you get involved with this, Monty, they might not grow up at all." Bolan described a few of the turkey doctors' masterpieces he'd seen in his war, ending with the man at the Capezzi House.

"I'm not backing out, Mr. Belasko. If somebody's pulling shit like that, all the more reason to put 'em down."

"Thanks, Monty. Now I can make that call."

DON PIETRO LISTENED, barely breathing, as the Shadow talked with the man who might be the Executioner.

"I'll come to the meeting on two conditions," the man said. "One is that I can come armed."

Don Pietro signaled with his hands. "Agree, but ask him to explain."

"That's no problem if you will answer one question."

"Why?"

"Exactly."

The other man's voice was level. "I trust you and Don Pietro. I hope I can trust all the other men who may be present, although I'd prefer that it be just the three of us." He spoke as if he were Brito's equal.

"It can be few. But—"

"Let me finish. I don't trust them as I trust the two of you. I'd prefer to be able to defend myself rather than force you to shoot an associate.

"Also, the secret of this meeting may leak out. In that case we might have uninvited guests."

"I can't argue with that. What's the other condition?"

"That a friend of mine can trail your car to the meeting place. It will be the discreet friend I've mentioned, and he need not attend the meet. But he has to know where it is and be where he can join the fight if there is one."

"If you can tell us how to recognize this man—"

"He'll be someone the Capezzis could never have hired. More than that, I won't tell you. Is that enough?"

Don Pietro nodded furiously, and the Shadow said, "Yes, Mr. Belasko. It's quite acceptable. Now, here is the time and place of our meeting...."

When the Shadow hung up, Don Pietro felt his heart fluttering in his thin chest. His breath came short, and his head swam at the thought of even trying to rise.

"Don Pietro!" the Shadow said. "Are you ill? Should I call for the doctor?"

"Should I go to the hospital the day before I begin my last battle? That's what you're asking, isn't it?"

"I suppose so."

"Well, suppose something else. Suppose that if this meet takes place, we can begin our final battle against Don Marco. We can even hope to win!"

"'Hope' is the word I'd use, too," the Shadow said with a frown. "I wish I knew who this 'friend' of Belasko's is."

"A wager, my friend. A case of wine that the friend is black."

"Why?"

"Not someone who would work for the Capezzis," Belasko said. You know what Don Marco thinks of the black people. He's too old to change, and if he's sleeping with those fools of the Silent Brotherhood..."

"The friend could also be Asian."

"True. It doesn't matter. Don Marco will go on thinking that the Silent Brotherhood is just another wolf who might share its prey. He won't see that they're mad dogs who might bite anyone."

"No, Don Pietro. But then Don Marco has always been something of a mad dog himself. Like attracts like."

7

"Mr. Belasko?"

The voice was unmistakable, even if it came from the dark interior of a pearl-gray Cadillac.

"Yes." The Executioner climbed into the car. He looked in the back seat, then at the driver. Even with the fading light, the mist and the dark interior, the man was dimmer than he should have been. The Shadow had really earned his name.

"There's no one in the back seat. If you wish me to open the trunk...?"

"As long as you're not carrying spare gas cans back there. They can be bad news if you're rear-ended."

"I know. We don't have that far to go tonight, in any case."

The Shadow put the car in gear, and they rolled down the driveway. Bolan relaxed, secretly keeping one eye on his watch. At the one-minute mark, he saw the Shadow stiffen slightly and something appear in the rearview mirror.

But the man's pride wouldn't let him doubt Bolan's word. He drove downhill in silence to the main road, then turned right, heading south.

Bolan used the time to check his weapons. He'd brought the Beretta without the shoulder stock but with several spare magazines; the Desert Eagle was secreted in his briefcase. The case also held four CS grenades and two M-26s, demolition and incendiary charges and assorted other surprises for the Brito Family if any treachery was planned tonight.

The Shadow put on a good act of keeping his eyes on the road. Bolan knew it was an act; a couple of times the Caddie's wheels hit the shoulder, and once the hitter nearly missed a turn. They took it on two wheels, burning rubber, and the man was sweating by the time the car steadied down again.

"I can take over if you want," Bolan suggested.

The Shadow's face twisted for a moment, as if he really wanted to push Bolan out of the car. Then he shook his head.

"Not necessary. I only hope that we're being tailed by your friend."

If Pelham was still hanging in there, he was a better tail driver than Bolan had expected. It might have been better to put one of Brognola's hand-picked people on the tailing job, but Pelham was on the spot. The fewer people who knew anything at this stage, the better.

"What kind of car?"

"A dark-colored BMW, I think."

Score one for the Shadow. "And the driver?"

"Black or wearing a dark ski mask."

"If it's not a ski mask, we're all right. And if it is a ski mask..." Bolan tapped the briefcase he'd just closed.

The Shadow nodded and slowed at a sign that read Passenger Ferry, 2 Miles. Then he turned left, away from the sign, and shifted up.

ONCE HE'D DECIDED that the tail was legitimate, the Shadow became a smooth, polished driver. The Cadillac rounded curves as if it were running on rails, climbed hills without slowing down and slipped down into valleys without a touch on the brakes.

Several times the rearview mirror turned up empty. Bolan could almost read the relief in the Shadow—and the frustration when the green BMW appeared again a few minutes later, as it always did.

The Shadow, Bolan decided, liked to be the best there was at *anything*. That made sense. If he hadn't been better than his enemies, the Shadow would have been dead years ago. Being the best had become a habit the man couldn't break.

In fact, Bolan could say the same thing about himself.

"Who is the man on our tail?" the Shadow asked.

"I didn't promise to tell you that," Bolan reminded.

"Will you?"

"No."

"It might help to be able to identify him in a fight."

"I'll tell you when the fight starts. *If* the fight starts while we're on the road."

The Shadow took a turn in silence. "Mr. Belasko, you aren't telling me very much."

Bolan gripped the dashboard and his temper. "Mr. Fieromosca, I think each of us is going to have a chance to learn about the other and the other's business. Plenty of chances, in fact, just by keeping our eyes and ears open and our mouths shut. I'm not going to stick my nose further into your business than that. You do the same."

"Don Pietro may ask more."

"If there's any chance of his asking more, this trip is wasted. Do we agree to keep our mouths shut, or do I get out right now?"

If the Shadow had stepped on the gas, he'd have been dead the next second. As it was, he slowed down, gripping the custom-molded rim of the steering wheel so hard that his knuckles stood out white against his olive skin.

Bolan looked in the rearview mirror. Pelham was back in place, as if he'd hooked an invisible wire to the Caddie's rear bumper.

The Shadow turned the car onto a gravel road and slowed. "We're nearly there, Mr. Belasko. I hope you won't expect an apology."

From the tone Bolan knew that was in fact intended as an apology. "No. You were only doing your duty to Don Pietro. I hope you'll allow me to do my duty as faithfully to *my* superiors."

"I will. I also promise to oppose anyone's keeping you from doing your duty."

"Except Don Pietro."

"Of course. You understand the ways of the Families well, Mr. Belasko."

"If I didn't, would I be of any use to you?"

In the darkness Bolan saw the Shadow smile. "Probably not." The Cadillac began to climb a hill. "Can you call your friend by radio?"

Bolan did have a miniature CB set locked to one frequency of the set in the BMW. But that was information he decided the Britos didn't need to have.

"No."

"Then I'll give you a pair of walkie-talkies. I'll stop, let you out and wait long enough for you to give one to your friend. Tell him to stay at least two hundred yards from the gate unless you call. Visibility is poor tonight, and we don't want any accidents to cast a shadow over our meet."

One of the Brito hardmen taking a shot at Monty Pelham would do more than cast a shadow. It would end the meet in a bloody shambles, which Bolan might not survive but the Britos certainly wouldn't.

"All right." The Cadillac stopped and Bolan climbed out. The moment he felt gravel under his feet, he dived into the shrubbery beside the road. Under cover he worked his way back three hundred yards to where Pelham had stopped. The security man was just climbing out of the BMW, a .44 Special Bulldog drawn, when Bolan popped up beside him.

"Jesus! It won't make the boss happy, him learning you gave me heart failure."

"So see a doctor." Bolan pulled the walkie-talkie from inside his windbreaker. The bushes were dripping wet, and his outer clothes were as soaked as if he'd been swimming.

"Take this and make sure you keep it in sight. But don't use it unless I say so."

"Our friends listening in?"

"In their place, wouldn't you?"

Pelham frowned. "Sounds like you started liking these people—" He broke off at the expression on Bolan's face.

"I like them as much as I ever did. But so far they seem to be playing this straight. I don't want to have to take them out tonight, either. That would leave Don Marco the biggest gun in the Seattle Families. We can do without that."

"And if Don Marco tries to crash the party?"

"That's what all the radios are for. If I shout 'party crashers' on either circuit, you get on the horn to Wolfshead. Report, then lock, load and come on in. I said I'd vouch for you."

"Sure you don't want me to be real sneaky? You might have noticed, I don't show up so good at night."

"Your being sneaky's going to make the Britos nervous. That's one thing we don't need."

Pelham slipped the walkie-talkie into a pocket of his bush jacket. As Bolan hit the bushes again, the man was pulling out an AR-15 and a pouch of loaded magazines from under the front seat.

THE EXECUTIONER and the capo of the Brito Family met in the greenhouse. After five minutes in its humid atmosphere, Bolan was even damper than before. He wasn't uncomfortable, however, and even if he had been he wouldn't have shown it. This wasn't the first time he'd dealt with the Families in psychological warfare, and he knew the rules. One of them wasn't to hint by word or movement that anything was wrong with their hospitality.

Don Pietro Brito half sat, half lay in a lounge chair, wearing a red dressing gown and blue pigskin slippers. He had clearly once been a powerful man, and now resented his body's failing before his mind did.

The Brito *consigliere* stood beside the lounge chair. He was the same age as Don Pietro and was bent with arthritis, but like his capo, still shrewd and alert. Bolan decided to dismiss the rumor that the *consigliere* was turning senile and held his post only because of old friendship with Don Pietro.

The Shadow lived up to his name, always on the move, hard to see, even harder to hear. From the pattern of his movements, Bolan guessed he was checking on guards posted around the greenhouse. Checking to see if they were on the alert, and also to make sure they weren't eavesdropping.

"Welcome to my house, Mr. Belasko. However this meeting ends, it will have been a pleasure to have you as my guest."

Bolan nodded. "I didn't expect anything else from Don Pietro Brito. Your reputation has gone before you."

"That's one of the prices of age," Don Pietro said. "One's reputation goes so far ahead that one's enemies are warned and lie in wait. I know now how a lion feels when his limbs stiffen and he hears the laughter of the hyena pack on his trail."

Bolan kept his lack of sympathy off his face. He hoped Don Pietro wouldn't waste too much of everybody's time, complaining that other men were trying to do to him what he'd done to the weak all his life.

"But I know you didn't come here to listen to an old man ramble." Don Pietro fixed his dark eyes on Bolan's face. "You came because you were curious about what enemies we had in common. Isn't that so?"

"Yes."

"I appreciate your honesty. I wouldn't indeed have blamed you if you didn't come. I can understand how it would be hard for you to believe that you and I have any enemies in common."

Bolan had the unpleasant feeling that Don Pietro was one jump ahead of him. Dominating this meeting was beginning to look not merely difficult but impossible.

"Good," Don Pietro said. "Now that we understand each other that much, I can do my duty as a host. You've had a long journey and are doubtless hungry and wet. May I do something about that?"

Accepting Don Pietro's hospitality wouldn't place Bolan under any obligations to the capo, or at least none that he recognized. It was accepting anything from such bloody hands that made Bolan's stomach knot.

The *consigliere*'s eyes hadn't left the Executioner's face since he entered the greenhouse. Now the older man frowned. He bent to whisper in Don Pietro's ear, but the capo shook his head.

"I will understand also, if you feel uneasy at accepting my hospitality. This will change nothing between us, for you have come under my roof. But surely a cup of coffee will harm nothing and no one?"

Certainly Don Pietro had one of the sharpest sets of wits that the Executioner had ever found in the Mafia. Bolan decided a cup of coffee would be a cheap price for the *consigliere*'s goodwill.

"Coffee, by all means," he said. "Black."

A silver pot and cups appeared on a brass tray. Don Pietro poured out two cups, then picked up one and drank from it himself. The *consigliere* cleared his throat.

Don Pietro's glare was that of an old wolf who still had teeth left, if not so many as he used to. "I think we can offer these little proofs that we can be trusted, without shame!"

"But the doctor—"

"I know what that son of a Milanese whore said about me and coffee! Well, I say to you that I sleep little enough as it is. One cup of coffee won't do me any harm."

Sight unseen, the doctor had Bolan's sympathy. He wouldn't want to try ordering Don Pietro Brito around, either. Fortunately his job wasn't to keep the Don in good health.

Bolan was halfway through his second cup of coffee when Don Pietro set down his cup and put both hands on the arms of his chair.

"If you will forgive me for coming so quickly to business . . . ?"

"Of course, Don Pietro. I realize that you're a busy man."

"Also an old one, who has twice as much to do and half the time in which to do it. Ah, well, nostalgia only wastes time.

"What I wish is very simple. For a million dollars I want you to destroy Don Marco Capezzi, his Family and his allies."

8

"So then what did you do?" Hal Brognola asked, curious.

"I was quiet just about as long as you were," Bolan replied.

"And then?"

"I was doing some fast thinking. I didn't want to refuse right away. I also didn't want to give them the impression that I thought the Don was crazy."

"I can see how that could strain their hospitality."

"Not the Don's, I suspect. But I wasn't so sure about the *consigliere* and Fieromosca."

Bolan quickly summarized the Don's situation as the man had described it. He wanted to retire, turning his turf and contacts over to a partnership of the Shadow and the *consigliere*. But he had a large amount of cash, and after providing his business heirs with a stake, he wanted the rest to go to his three daughters.

The other Seattle Families, represented by Don Marco Capezzi, opposed this. They wanted the money paid to them as the price of leaving the Shadow and the *consigliere* with the territory. Since Don Pietro had already involved his blood relations, Don Marco had decided the best warning was to take out Sam Brito.

Brognola sounded skeptical. "Sounds like the Britos know a lot they're not telling."

"No argument. But I'm coming to that."

The cash Don Pietro wanted to leave to his daughters added up to about ten million dollars, safely laundered. A million to Bolan would leave three million for each daughter.

"Fine. Now for the big question. What did you say?"

"I said that I'd have to consult with my superiors. I couldn't commit them without that. I added that I knew there'd be at least two conditions. One of them was mine—that the Shadow works with me."

"I see. Cutting off their deniability?"

"Right. I'm not going to let the Shadow take over as Don Leon without his lifting a gun to get there. I don't think he was too happy about that, at least not at first. Then the *consigliere* and Don Pietro both stared him down. He sort of grumbled and agreed."

"About what I'd expect of the man," Brognola said. "What's the other condition?"

"Everything they know about any connection between the Capezzis and the Silent Brotherhood, they pass on to us. Not being a name-dropper, I didn't mention Corporal Goss. I just said we had evidence that the two might be working together. If so, we might have a bigger fight on our hands than we'd expected, and we both might need some extra help."

"What did they say to that?"

"The Shadow sort of shrugged. Don Pietro was gung ho, so that settled it. I left the old man with the idea that maybe we'd rather have the Silent Brotherhood than the million dollars."

"That's no lie," Brognola said. "Particularly if they're snooping around nuke dumps." Bolan heard his friend putting down a cup, and his chair creaking as he stretched. Then his voice returned.

"So. How do you see it?"

"Unless my accepting would mess up any operations you have on tap..."

"You'll go?"

"Yeah. We'll learn a lot more about the Seattle Families than they'll learn about us. That's worth more than ten million dollars we probably couldn't get our hands on anyway. If we track down the Silent Brotherhood, as well, you name the price."

"I can't count that high," Brognola said. "Have you got the Brito file?"

"I picked it up on the way back. Monty Pelham dropped me off."

"Okay. Read the file before you decide, and remember one thing. If I know you, the most you'll do for Don Pietro and the Shadow is to take them last, right?"

"Got it."

"If they know who you are, they'll know it, too. The Shadow is a bad man to have at your back, knowing that."

"I know. But I'm just as bad, and I'll be at his back as much as he's at mine. Sleep on that."

"What's sleep? I've got an operation to clear."

"And I've got a file the size of *War and Peace* to go through. So let's get to work."

THE BRITO FILE WASN'T quite as long as *War and Peace*. More like the length of an average paperback novel. It wasn't happy reading, either. As he worked through it, Bolan felt rage ebb and flow through him until it settled into a frozen ball in the pit of his stomach.

Don Pietro Brito was a gifted man. The file told Bolan that a dozen times over, starting with his having a college degree in chemistry. The warrior knew of less than half a dozen mafiosi of Brito's generation who'd gone to college.

The details didn't matter. The general picture did. It added up to something that Bolan knew existed, had even met, but never expected to work with—a man who could have made a bigger fortune than he had now, in any one of several fields. Or if not made more money, at least made a comfortable living and not have had to worry about Mafia Dons wanting him to leave his money to them.

Don Pietro had *wanted* to be a Mafia Don.

His three daughters were all married, with children of their own; one was a lawyer, one a painter and one a housewife. Their husbands were a doctor, a lawyer and a successful thriller writer.

Apparently Don Pietro was a doting grandfather. Bolan could believe that he'd learned the risks of a criminal career and wanted to spare his grandchildren from them. But if he'd learned that so well, why couldn't he have avoided crime in the first place?

Hindsight was always futile with one's own actions; with other people's it was just plain silly. Bolan knew he was more upset by Don Pietro's file than he should have been, or he wouldn't have been dwelling on what couldn't be helped.

Anyway, the seven grandchildren were certainly innocent. They had as much right to the blood money as anybody, and if someday they learned where it came from and wanted to pay it back—that was their choice.

Something thumped on the roof, about as loud as a snowball. As Bolan looked up, he heard a sharp pop, then a long hiss like the grandfather of all snakes and a faint but angry rumble.

He didn't need to wait to smell smoke to know that someone had just punched a fire bomb through the roof of the safehouse.

Bolan hadn't unpacked anything but the Beretta, Desert Eagle and a few clothes. In seconds he was moving out. He wasn't going to leave anything behind, not even a scrap of paper from the Brito file. The house might not burn completely. Even if it did, somebody could be waiting, ready to dart in and do a quick search just ahead of the flames.

Somebody was certainly waiting outside, gun in hand. As Bolan reached the ground floor, three shots smashed through the dining-room window. Aimed only at his shadow, they went wide.

Bolan shifted position, deliberately trying to draw fire while he pulled out the Desert Eagle. The Beretta might not have enough stopping power.

Muzzle-flashes gave away one man's position. The Executioner waited until the bullets stopped shredding curtains and shattering glass. Then he vaulted the railing and landed, feet crunching glass, the big .44 Magnum up and ready.

The slugs from the big pistol flung the gunman out from behind his bush, over a wheelbarrow and onto another bush. The second bush hid a comrade, loyal but careless. He revealed his position by reaching up to help his friend.

Then he flew backward, hands tangled in his friend's clothes, as the Desert Eagle roared again. Two ski-masked figures rolled out from behind the shrub, one thrashing around wildly.

Bolan flung his equipment through the shattered window and followed close behind. He landed spring-legged, crouched with the .44 ready for action, but found neither targets nor enemies. Only two men had been deployed, at least for this side of the house.

It wasn't the whole hit team, as Bolan learned a moment later. A figure in green fatigues sprinted around the house, toting a mini-Uzi. He might have got lucky; what he got instead was trigger freeze, followed by a .44 bullet that took off the top of his head.

A fourth man sprinted for a compact car parked in the driveway. He was moving too fast for Bolan to get a precise bead on him. Nothing else would do for a target this close to the street.

Bolan lowered the Eagle's muzzle, and the next bullet slammed into the car's engine compartment. The compact lifted on two wheels, slammed back down and caught fire. The fleeing man ducked behind it, threw a wild shot at Bolan, then dashed out into the street.

A moment later he returned, flying completely over the privet hedge and crashing to the grass almost at Bolan's feet. His chest was completely crushed, and his head was nearly at right angles to his shoulder.

Bolan hastily reloaded the .44 and didn't holster it until he saw Monty Pelham walking up the driveway.

The security man knelt beside his victim and stripped off the ski mask.

The man's features were horribly twisted but strongly Asian. Bolan looked from the dead man to Pelham.

"You don't seem surprised."

"Tell you about it on the road. You ready to head out?"

"It beats having the police haul us off for questioning."

Pelham got them out of there, and when they reached Highway 167, the security man relaxed and explained.

"Mr. Leung called the boss. Said he'd picked up rumors of a hit by the Tongs. Didn't seem like they knew what he was really up to, but they didn't like and they wanted him to stop it."

"Maybe. But those four were shooting pretty freely, if it was just supposed to be a torch job."

"Didn't say it was. Anyway, the boss called me, and I snagged some wheels and rolled on down. Looks like you had the situation pretty well in hand, though."

"You might say that." Then Bolan added, "But I don't know about all the other situations. You know this turf. How far do we need to go to make a couple of nice quiet phone calls?"

BOLAN MADE HIS CALLS from the back room of a quiet bar about ten miles south along 167. One call was to Hal Brognola; the other was to the number he'd been given for the Britos.

After that he ate his first regular meal in several days, but the food tasted like sawdust. He wanted to be up and at enemies, starting with the Capezzis.

He slept at Pelham's apartment, and in the morning the situation, if not the weather, started looking brighter. Brognola didn't call, but the man who did was a Stony Man operative Bolan knew. Justice had nothing going down in the area, so all was clear for Bolan to "work" with the Britos against the other Seattle Families.

The warrior dialed the Brito number, and Fieromosca answered on the third ring.

"What's the word?"

Bolan told him and the other man laughed. "This calls for a drink, *after* our first win. I thought you'd say yes, so I chose our target."

Bolan didn't like the overconfidence or not having been consulted, but replied, "Where's that?"

"At a warehouse used by the Blue Lily Tong. They're the ones who tried the hit yesterday. Our sources are firm on that."

"I see." Bolan saw quite a lot and didn't like much of it. The Shadow might be lying, trying to divert Bolan into a private war against the Tongs. Even if he was telling the truth, where had he learned the name of the Tong?

"If the Tongs are in the field against us, we have to knock them back before we can fight the Capezzis without watching our back," the Shadow continued. "Also, one of Don Marco's allies or at least one of Don Pietro's enemies might have arranged the hit with the Blue Lilies."

It was only too possible, mafiosi and Tong soldiers both being what they were.

"Mr. Belasko," the Shadow said, "do you need to talk with your superiors over every change in our battle plan? If that's so, I can see serious problems in our working together."

The Mafia hitter really sounded concerned. But concerned for the failure of some secret plan, or concerned like any good professional about not wasting time when you faced fast-moving enemies?

Bolan decided to gamble. He'd come too far to back out without losing all the ground he'd gained and more. Even if he could afford to leave the Capezzis alone, there was still the Silent Brotherhood, and there Brognola really wanted some action.

He'd get it, even if the way to it led through the Seattle Tongs.

"The Tongs it will be, then," Bolan agreed.

Fieromosca named a rendezvous and suggested equipment that either he or Bolan should provide, then hung up.

Pelham looked at Bolan eagerly.

"Sorry to disappoint you, Monty. But you hang back for the next few days. The deal was for just me and the Shadow. If I bring a sidekick, he'll want one, too. Right now the fewer the better. Besides, we need someone to keep an eye on Torstensson."

"You think the bad guys might try to take him out?"

"I'm sure somebody in the police department leaked the Tongs' identity where somebody on the Britos' payroll heard it. What happens if somebody hears about the policemen feeding information to your boss?"

"Any rough stuff against the boss gets Boeing pissed off at the Capezzis," Pelham said. "Not too smart in this town."

"Don Marco doesn't think that way," Bolan pointed out. "You sneeze at a Sicilian, and he'll want your blood."

"They really think like that?"

"The blood feud used to be their national sport." Bolan knew all about the historical origins of that particular bad habit. In this case, to understand all wasn't to forgive all. Bad habits, unlike good whiskey, didn't improve with age.

"Okay. I'll hang in there with the boss at least until he's got both arms back in action. But I don't have to like it. There's something that smells funny about this case."

Bolan nodded. Pelham was right. Of course, dealing with the Mafia was like working in a garbage dump. Bad smells were part of the deal. But Bolan's instincts told him that more than the usual criminal garbage was making a stink here.

9

"These are the builder's plans," Fieromosca said as he spread the photocopies on the table. "The warehouse has passed through four owners since it was built, but I couldn't get anything more recent."

Bolan nodded. Four owners could mean fifty to seventy years and enough changes to make the plans outdated and the warehouse a death trap for people who didn't know their way around it.

"Since that means we'll be acting on incomplete information, I want to keep things simple," the Shadow continued. "Onto the roof, in through the skylight and set the firebombs. If there's an office with records that might be useful, we hit that. No shooting until we're on the way out, if possible. Even then, we shoot only people who get in our way."

This time Bolan shook his head. "Only people who are shooting at us."

"You want to give them the first shot?"

"If we're as good as we think we are, why not? Even at night, we might find innocent warehouse workers. Or people who work for the Tongs but not on the criminal side, because it's better than the streets."

"Your standards and mine are different," the Shadow said in a flat, almost bland tone. Bolan couldn't tell if he disapproved or not.

"I'm sure they are," he replied in the same tone. "I'm also sure we have to work together in spite of it. There won't be a problem with our being recognized, not with our masks. We're too big for Asians, but I thought we were supposed to be Capezzi hitters."

"We are."

"Then the more witnesses to our act the better. Besides," Bolan added with a grin, "there's the ammo problem. Are you planning on taking a third man as ammo bearer?"

The Shadow looked confused and suspicious. "No."

"Then we're going to be right down on the minimum load for this kind of job. If the Tongs have as many soldiers as I suspect, we'll need every round for them. We won't have any to waste on janitors and stock boys."

"Okay, I'll concede the point. On this job, at least."

They anchored the builder's plans with ashtrays and empty glasses and went to work. Apart from the problem of shooting innocents, the Shadow had worked things out very well. Bolan's instincts that he was working with a highly competent professional grew stronger.

The same instincts also told him that the Shadow was playing hidden games. Did he really not care about innocents? Did he want to provoke a war between the Capezzis and Seattle's Chinese community? Or was he just pretending ruthlessness to draw Bolan out?

The Executioner decided that all of these questions needed answers, but not now. They had a battle to plan.

"Do we want to blow the other skylights to give the fire more ventilation when we start? Or will the doors be better?"

The Shadow pulled out a magnifying glass and held it over the doors. "If they haven't been changed around, the doors would give a better draft...."

THE FENCE around the warehouse was new, steel mesh on I-bar supports topped with a coil of razor wire. Bolan saw no connections or insulators for electrifying the wire.

Bolan studied the warehouse loading area and saw nothing moving, human or animal. He nodded to the Shadow.

Wearing a blacksuit similar to Bolan's and a ski mask, loaded with weapons, the Mafia hitter could have been Bolan's twin. A close look would have shown that he was thicker through the body and shorter in the legs, but nobody was likely to get that close a look tonight and live to tell about it.

Bolan scrambled up one of the supports and started on the razor wire with insulated cutters. It parted easily enough, and he'd just made a man-size gap when the dogs appeared.

They ran out from under the loading dock, barking furiously. The Shadow went down on one knee, and his silenced .22 snapped up. Bolan heard three *phuts* and an agonized yelp, and both dogs were down. One was still writhing and whimpering pitifully.

It was still whimpering as the two men scrambled down the inside of the fence and headed for the warehouse. Bolan stopped by the dog and drew his Gerber.

"What . . . ?" the Shadow began.

"I won't leave it like that."

"Don't blame you."

Seconds later the two men scrambled up the access ladder beside the loading dock and were crouching behind the cornice when the first guard appeared. Bolan watched him sweep the loading area with his flashlight, then saw the beam come to rest on the two dead dogs.

The guard pulled out a radio and a whistle, which he blew furiously, then started talking urgently into the radio. At the same time Bolan heard the Shadow call.

"Fire in the hole!"

The warrior flattened himself on the roof as the charge of C-4 plastique took out the nearest skylight. Bits of glass, rusty metal bars and wire pattered down on the tarpaper. Bolan rose to his knees, then hit the floor again as he saw the Shadow throw three grenades.

Each grenade was on target, smashing through the glass of one of the remaining skylights. Just below the roof level, the grenades exploded. The skylights vanished in sprays of glass and metal, but most of the blast and shrapnel would be directed downward.

The Executioner was unrolling his climbing rope when a man's head rose over the cornice, followed by a .357 Redhawk. The Beretta spit three rounds, and the gunner's face became a red ruin and vanished.

A cry floated up from below, and Bolan heard two bodies thud onto the concrete. The guard must have knocked a friend off the ladder, and both had gone down together.

But the Shadow had already hooked his rope to the rim of one skylight. The warrior had no time to check his rear if he didn't want the Shadow to lead the way. That could leave the hitter free to shoot as he pleased, innocent and guilty alike.

He could also shoot only the men dangerous to him, leaving the rest to make target practice on Bolan coming down his rope alone. "Accidents" like this had happened in too many firefights.

Bolan hooked his rope on the least rusty section of skylight rim, holstered the Beretta and swung down into the darkness. He was in midair when the Shadow touched down and promptly threw a flashbang grenade that exploded just where the Executioner intended to land.

The concussion snapped Bolan's hook loose from the battered skylight rim. He dropped ten feet, but landed with the Beretta in hand. He thought for a moment that he'd landed on a corpse. A second touch told him that it was only a pile of old mattresses.

But there were two corpses in sight as his eyes adjusted to the dimness inside the warehouse. Fortunately for the Shadow, both of them were adult male Asians, and both of them were armed. Bolan scooped up an Ingram and an anonymous 9 mm automatic, then called for the Shadow.

The call drew a blast of automatic fire from Bolan's left, badly aimed but noisy. He couldn't quite place the shooter, but another trick might work.

Bolan let out a convincing scream, the cry of a badly wounded man. By the time bullets stopped pinging off the walls and floor, he heard nearing footsteps.

So did the Shadow, who fired a withering blast into the approaching men. One of them went down, hit by bullets that passed so close to Bolan that he felt their wind. The other two closed in. The warrior shifted position to clear the Shadow's line of fire and get some protection from a pile of empty crates.

One of the men seemed to want to go hand-to-hand. He leaped high, and Bolan shot him in midair. His leap blocked his friend's shot. Bolan rolled out from behind the crates, and the Beretta put two 3-round bursts into the second man.

Bolan was back behind the crate and reloading the Beretta when the Shadow spoke.

"I found two more bodies when I came down, and hit another one. He's left a blood trail, but I think he's out of it. Let's set the bombs and split."

"Fine. I'll check these crates for something that'll—"

Bolan broke off. From the darkness toward the rear of the warehouse, he heard scuffling. Voices, too, at least one speaking in Chinese and one unmistakably in Vietnamese.

Then a cry for help in accented English.

The Shadow might have read Bolan's mind. Another flashbang arced into the middle of the warehouse, lighting up the whole interior—and two men standing over a third by an elevator door. The two men gaped and were shot down where they stood.

Bolan reached the man who'd cried out first. He knew that meant exposing his back to the Shadow. He also knew the Shadow didn't speak a word of Vietnamese.

The man on the floor was gasping out his life, with blood trickling from his mouth. He was gray haired, but not too old to be angry at seeing his hopes of a better life in America fading away.

"Who are these men, father?" he asked, in the old man's native tongue.

"Bad...bad Chinese. Bring from ship. Hiding down below..." The man seemed determined to use the last of his strength to speak English.

"Where down below?"

"Come up in elevator. You come shooting. Others go back down. I ... I fight. Not get away..."

His voice trailed off, and for a moment the trickle of blood became a gush. Then it stopped, and so did the old man's breath.

Bolan was feeling a thin wrist for a pulse when the Shadow came up behind him. "Who's the papa-san?"

"I think he's one of a party of boat people the Tongs have been trying to smuggle in. Or maybe out. Anyway, I think there are more of them down below."

"What are we, the Red Cross?"

Bolan noted that the Shadow knew what his partner had in mind, even if he might not approve.

"The Red Cross is a noncombatant organization. We aren't."

"Also we're here and the Red Cross isn't."

"I somehow have the feeling we agree."

They set four incendiary charges with twenty-minute fuses, then put a charge with a one-minute fuse in the elevator. Bolan estimated that they'd reach the bottom of the stairs just as it went off.

He was only seconds off, not enough to matter. The charge blew open the elevator door and flattened several Tong soldiers. Not all of them were dead when they went down, but all of them were dead when Bolan and his partner moved on.

They raced through a dimly lit maze of mostly empty rooms. Some of them showed signs of recent habitation, including wrist and leg irons hanging from rusty chains.

Where the builder's plan had shown a partial wall, Bolan found a complete one. A flashlight revealed twenty feet of new brickwork, and an even newer steel door set in the bricks.

"Cover me," he said. "I'm going to blow the lock."

"Why not the door?"

"If the boat people are still in the building, they're behind this door."

Bolan needed that cover. He'd just finished placing the stick of C-4 when Tong reinforcements stormed down the stairs. They had more firepower and determination than marksmanship, but there were a lot of them and that meant a lot of bullets.

Fortunately Tong marksmanship wasn't the only thing that was poor. Their communications left a lot to be desired, as well. The guards inside the door apparently thought that all the shooting meant their friends had things in hand.

They opened the door—just as the C-4 went off.

One Tong guard simply disintegrated. Another flew as high as the basement ceiling would let him, then crashed down with his skull flattened and one arm ruined. Bolan kicked the twisted, smoking door open and charged in.

He found only one target. A guard stood backed against the wall, firing desperately into a seething mass of human flesh. The mass churned, spit out a naked man with his face a bloody mess who lurched toward the guard.

He had just enough time to fire the last shot in his revolver before Bolan cut him down. Then the warrior had to back away to avoid being knocked down by the boat people surging forward to make sure that the last Tong soldier was dead.

The Vietnamese were just starting to realize that the fight was over when two grenades exploded outside. Bolan whirled, then saw the Shadow storm through the door and slam the undamaged inner door behind him.

"Those were my last two. I thought I'd better keep their heads down while I joined you. What next?"

Bolan didn't mind being conceded the leadership. His answer came quickly.

"First aid for the wounded."

Five of the seventeen Vietnamese had bullet wounds. Only one looked dangerous, and none of the four children was even scratched. In five minutes the

Vietnamese were convinced that their rescuers were just that.

The only problem was that the rescuers had only seven minutes left to get the Viets out of the warehouse before it went up in flames. That included time to fight their way through the remaining Tong soldiers, climb the stairs and reach the doors.

Bolan had a gut feeling that there wasn't going to be enough time.

He holstered the Beretta, raised the flashlight and began to search the room. Toward the rear he found a low dark opening. He drew the Beretta again, held the flashlight between his teeth and began a low crawl through the wall.

What he'd expected to be a tunnel was hardly more than a door. On the other side, though, was a tunnel—one with saltwater lapping at a patch of mud and shingle, where three small boats lay. Two of them had outboard motors.

At the far end of the tunnel the flashlight showed camouflage netting.

Bolan crawled back into the room.

"Three minutes to go," the Shadow announced.

"I don't think we have a problem anymore." Bolan described the tunnel.

"Makes sense," the hitter replied. "This warehouse used to be built out over the water. Then they filled in under it. All the Tongs would have had to do was dig out the fill and hide the entrance. Then they'd have a nice little hidden back door."

"Which is going to come in handy for us tonight." Bolan turned to the refugees and spoke in Vietnamese.

"We're going to take you out in the boats. We don't have far to go, and the water is calm. The women and children will go in the two boats with motors."

The surprise on the Vietnamese faces was unmistakable. No doubt the Tongs had them drugged aboard ship and smuggled ashore unconscious. Bolan wondered briefly what Chinese Tongs were planning to do with Vietnamese refugees who probably didn't have fifty dollars among them. Then he decided to kick that one upstairs to Hal Brognola.

Right now Mack Bolan's business was living up to his second Army nickname—Sergeant Mercy.

He had all the Vietnamese in the tunnel by the time the charges upstairs went off. He had half of them in the boats when he heard a second, more violent series of explosions. The ceiling of the tunnel quivered, and so did the water as the shock wave passed through it. The long rumble that followed the concussion seemed to go on forever.

All the Vietnamese started to talk, cry, shout or scream at once.

"Quiet!" Bolan yelled. "The only way to safety is out the tunnel. So get back in the boats and sit still!"

The Shadow disappeared back into the main room, then came back spitting dust.

"Something upstairs blew and dumped half the floor into the basement. I don't think we have to worry about those Tong soldiers anymore. Now, if these gooks will just stay cool—"

"Watch your language. Some of them might understand English."

The hitter stared at Bolan, opened his mouth to speak, then shut it in silence. Still silent, he squatted in the stern of the motorless boat, unslung his G-3 and began adjusting the night sight.

Two minutes later the convoy was under way, Bolan in the lead boat towing the motorless one. The last boat was in the charge of a man who said he'd been both a fisherman and an officer in the South Vietnamese navy.

The ceiling of the tunnel was steel plate. Bolan saw joints gaping and sand and mud trickling down as the boats approached the end of the tunnel. Another major-caliber blast upstairs, and the whole lash-up was likely to come down on their heads.

What came down instead was the camouflage netting. The blast jerked it loose from its rusty supports, and it slithered down on the last boat. Shouts and curses turned into cries of terror as people felt the weight of the net dragging the boat over.

"Sit still, you piles of ox dung!" Bolan heard the Vietnamese officer screaming. The cries subsided. So did the whirr of the outboard motor.

"Someone in the stern, lift the net free of the propeller!" was the next order. Someone obeyed. By now Bolan understood what the man was up to. He maneuvered his own boat so that he and the Shadow could each grab one side of the net.

Then the Vietnamese opened his throttle and his boat shot out from under the net. It hit a wave, bounced, recovered, then was clear of the tunnel and heading out into open water.

Bolan opened the throttle of his outboard motor and drew the Beretta. The rest of the convoy surged out of the tunnel in the other boat's wake.

The warehouse was now blazing from basement to roof. Flames shot out of all four skylights, both doors and several gaps in the wall. Whatever the Tongs had stored there was highly flammable, and some of it must have been explosive.

As if to prove that again, another blast punched Bolan's eardrums. The entire seaward wall of the warehouse shivered, then crumbled in a roar of falling masonry. Spray leaped up as high as a house when the masonry plunged into the water.

When the water and smoke cleared away, the entrance to the tunnel was buried ten feet deep under the tons of stone.

"You *like* that kind of narrow escape?" the Shadow grumbled as he saw Bolan's grim smile.

"Consider the alternative." Bolan turned the boat's bow seaward. He wanted to get a mile or two offshore as fast as possible to be clear of the police and firemen. Then he'd head to where he could drop off the Vietnamese so they could get medical care. He and the Shadow could then go on their way.

"How is Nguyen doing?" he called.

A chorus of voices said that Nguyen was conscious and not bleeding anymore. Good. If the worst of the wounds didn't start bleeding again, he'd make it.

"Look!"

Bolan turned, his gaze following a thin pointing arm. He frowned.

A forty-foot cabin cruiser was coming up in the wake of the convoy. It seemed to have several men on deck, and a searchlight was sweeping the water ahead of it.

"Are they following us?" Bolan asked.

"I think so. I also think that's the boat they used to carry us from the big ships to the little boats. The drugs didn't make all of us sleep. Some of us saw more than they wanted us to."

"You've all seen too much tonight," Bolan replied. "So we'll just have to finish what we began." He frowned again. "Do you speak Chinese?"

"Well enough to keep those sons of bitches confused for a minute or two."

"Good. Tell them that these boats are carrying people who died of an unknown plague. You and your soldiers are taking them to sea to dump them."

"But then they will not come close!" the Vietnamese protested.

"They don't need to," the Shadow told him as he pulled on his mask. The Vietnamese began lying down. Last of all the Shadow lay down on top of them, pulling rags over his G-3.

By the time Bolan had his ski mask on, the cruiser was less than fifty yards astern. The searchlight swept back and forth, then finally came to rest on Bolan's boat. A moment later he heard a shout from the boat's flying bridge, and its engines roared into higher gear.

The cruiser overtook the convoy in the next minute, then slowed to ride alongside. From the bridge a man with a loud-hailer called in Chinese.

"What are you doing out here? The warehouse is on fire!"

"I know nothing of that," the Vietnamese replied in the same language. "I only know that these people are dead or dying of a plague I've never seen. My orders were to take them out to sea and cast them adrift."

Bolan couldn't understand most of the conversation that followed. He did hear the word "plague" repeated several times. He also saw the Tong soldiers edging farther away from the railing each time.

Finally the man with the loud-hailer seemed to reach a decision. He gave sharp orders and pointed astern. Two of the deckhands began coiling lines to heave over to the boats.

Bolan knew the Shadow was alert and watching for a signal. The Executioner decided it was time. Towed astern, the boats would be out of easy reach of the cruiser. Then, sooner or later, someone aboard would remember to ask for the Blue Lily Tong passwords....

The warrior raised the Beretta and drilled a triburst into the man with the loud-hailer. The four men on the deck died from a burst of 7.62 mm NATO rounds, half a magazine sent their way on full automatic.

The other four were underfoot, but dead or dying, as Bolan and the Shadow leaped aboard. In the pilothouse a man turned, and both boarders shot him out of his seat. Another man appeared in the companionway, and Bolan took him out with a quick burst to the chest. Then the Shadow was leaping below, slinging his G-3 and drawing his Hi-Power for the close-quarters work.

Bolan leaned over the railing and shouted to the Vietnamese officer to get his people aboard the cruiser as fast as possible.

The frail Vietnamese possessed unexpected strength. They were aboard in minutes. As the last one sat down, the Shadow came back on deck.

"All clear below," he reported, and slipped a fresh magazine into his G-3. "Let's get out of here."

Bolan nodded and climbed the ladder to the bridge. He'd just taken the wheel when he heard the Shadow cursing. "What's the matter?"

"I just realized I forgot to leave a sign that this was a Capezzi hit! We were supposed to get the Tongs and the Capezzis mad at each other."

The Executioner felt relief. The man could have told him before, but there was no harm done. And this time, at least, no treachery intended.

"Haven't you ever heard of telephones?"

The Shadow struck his forehead with the palm of his hand. "*Disgrazia!* Where are my wits?"

"Why don't you go look for them while I head us for that telephone? The Viets will need to call a doctor and the police while we clear out."

Bolan swung the wheel to port and opened the throttles. The cruiser's wake rose white at the stern, and it heeled over as it turned.

He and the Shadow had wrecked the Blue Lily Tong, saved seventeen innocent lives and started a lot of rumors flying around Seattle's underworld.

That was a good start, but it was only a start. This nightmare in the Northwest was a major battle, and tonight was just the first successful skirmish.

10

A thousand yards from shore Bolan turned off the cruiser's lights. A hundred yards from shore he throttled the diesels back. The Vietnamese officer stood on the bow, ready to heave a line ashore.

With one eye on the fathometer, Bolan let the cruiser creep in toward the shore. A sudden hiss, and the line was snaking through the air into the bushes ashore. It caught, and the officer braced his legs as he started hauling in.

The boat's keel finally touched muddy bottom, and Bolan and the Shadow jumped ashore. Then the warrior unwound the line, threw it back aboard the cruiser and waved to the officer who now stood on the bridge.

"Thank you," the Vietnamese called. "May Buddha smile on your fight."

The diesels rumbled in reverse, and the darkened cruiser faded into the night. The Shadow picked himself up and asked, "Why did we bring the cruiser inshore instead of hopping into one of the boats right off?"

"The cover story they're going to tell needs all three of the boats. If one turns up missing, they're going to get hassled."

"I suppose so. God knows they don't need any more."

They set off uphill toward where the map showed a road. Bolan took the lead, and they were out of sight of the water before he remembered that there was a Mafia hit man at his back.

Remembering that was a shock. So was realizing that he'd been giving the Shadow advice the same way he gave it to Monty Pelham or anyone else. For a moment the Shadow had been just another man with talent but not quite as much experience as the Executioner.

That was true, but not the whole truth. The Shadow was still a professional killer for the Mafia; he'd never be somebody to relax with, even after a mission. *Especially* after a mission, when he might decide that his partner's usefulness was over, or that his partner had decided the same about him....

They reached a public telephone half an hour later. Bolan stood outside keeping watch while the Shadow made his calls. The Executioner would have liked to listen in. That would only give the man an excuse to listen to his, though.

Hal Brognola was nowhere to be found. More than likely he was catching up on lost sleep. He usually put in an eighteen-hour day when he was setting up a mission for Bolan or any of the other Stony Man teams.

Now that the mission was launched, he'd rest up to be ready for any emergencies that cropped up.

An hour later they were heading into town in a "borrowed" Ford pickup. As they turned off I-5 toward the university, the Shadow lit a cigarette.

"You got any big ideas about what we do next?" he said.

"We've got the Tongs off balance and suspicious," Bolan replied. "It won't hurt to keep them that way. You're sure you can convince them this was a Capezzi hit?"

"Don Marco's going to be the biggest suspect. The next biggest'll be the Viets. That might get some of them wasted."

"I've made some arrangements to take care of that."

"I suppose you won't give me any details?"

"Not unless you tell me how you pretended to be a Capezzi."

"I would, but I think you've got a weak stomach."

"Not weak, just empty." There was something to be said for regular meals, even on a job. At least there was when you weren't in the jungle or some other place where you were lucky to eat at all.

Over hamburgers at a truck stop they exchanged ideas, and it didn't take long to find they were both of the same mind.

"We wait just long enough to make it look right, then we imitate Tongs hitting the Capezzis," the Shadow said. "A couple of small hits first, then we try for something big. If we can't get Don Marco ready to shit his pants in a week, I'm going to retire and raise tomatoes like Don Pietro."

Bolan nodded. Every one of those hits would tell him more about the Capezzi Family. Some of it the Feds or the local police already knew, but not all.

For now, the mission was going to be a "Heads the Executioner wins, tails the Families lose" situation. The longer it stayed that way, the better.

DON MARCO CAPEZZI'S FACE was flushed red and twisted with rage.

Antonio Pescaglia looked at his furious capo more coldly than usual. If Don Marco was going to charge about like a mad bull, maybe it would be better if he had a stroke and died.

Maybe not, also. The old man had no recognized heir. Pescaglia fancied that in a straightforward fight he'd be able to take over, but any kind of fight would divide the Family in the face of the enemy.

Also, it would be a fool's dream to believe that the fight could be straightforward. None of Pescaglia's rivals would be so treacherous as to seek aid from the Tongs. But some might approach the Britos, and Don Pietro would welcome them with open arms, as well as open purses and an open hand with weapons and ammunition—as long as they were used only on *his* enemies.

"Those yellow bastards!" the capo raged. It was the mildest slur he'd used against the Tongs for some time. "How dare they call anything they will do to us a war? I've had more trouble scratching fleas!"

"Enough fleas, and you spend all your time scratching," Pescaglia said mildly. "Then you have no time to fight larger enemies."

"Such as the Britos?"

"I thought we hadn't finished with them."

Don Marco glared. "Your tone is insolent, Antonio." He didn't order his chief soldier to stand, but Pescaglia made the gesture anyway.

"Don Marco, if I have offended you, it's only out of concern for our victory. We didn't, I admit, plan on fighting the Tongs, as well as the Britos.

"On the other hand, the Mangnanis have been asking to join us. On your orders I suggested that we were strong enough to fight the Britos ourselves."

"We were," Don Marco agreed, his rage now fading to a sour look. "We had no need to admit them to our councils, teach them our secrets or divide Brito's money when we took it."

"But now, Don Marco?"

"Now you may meet with Don Ettore and whoever he calls his chief soldier these days. Contamine, I think. Suggest that it might be worth their while to make some of their soldiers ready to work with ours. Under your command, of course."

"Of course," Pescaglia said.

Pescaglia pretended to be loyal, even calm, during the rest of the meeting. But he was grinning the moment he knew he was out of Don Marco's sight.

One way of strengthening his own position was recruiting other Families' soldiers. But to do that secretly, without Don Marco's permission, would be suspicious. A single word to Don Marco, and Pescaglia would end his life on a meat hook, with wire cutting off his wind, blood and manhood.

That would ruin the Capezzis' chances in their fight with the Britos, of course. But that wouldn't help a dead man, and Don Marco would think of vengeance on a traitor before anything else.

Now, though, Pescaglia had his capo's permission to recruit other Families' soldiers. He'd start tonight, and in three days all should be ready.

He decided that he'd spend the fourth day celebrating with a visit to Sally's. She had a new girl, and the rumors about her were exciting. Even if they were all nonsense, there was always good old reliable Gloria.

THREE DAYS, three hits.

On the first day it was a Capezzi bookmaking operation. Bolan didn't even draw his gun. He merely stood in the background, ski-masked and grim, while the Shadow herded the clerks out into the street. A match to the flash-paper records was the only ammunition they used, and they left a nice blaze behind.

On the second day they hit a bar where Capezzi soldiers met to pick up girls and get drunk. Bolan covered the barroom with an Uzi while the Shadow stripped the bar of cash. He also stripped the bartender of courage, but stopped short of pistol-whipping him.

Just to increase the confusion, the two men had memorized an exchange in Mandarin. Tong soldiers over six feet tall weren't unknown, and with their faces masked, all anyone would remember was their speaking Chinese.

"Too bad there weren't any Capezzi soldiers around when we hit," the Shadow said afterward. "Wasting a couple more would have made the whole job a lot more convincing."

"We might have wasted a few peaceful patrons in the process," Bolan reminded his partner. "Then we'll have everybody, not just the Capezzis, chasing the Tongs."

The Shadow nodded. He was now willing to listen to practical arguments for not wiping out innocent people. But then Bolan had never really suspected him of being one of those mafiosi who loved the sight of blood and the sound of agonized screams. He killed efficiently, coldly and thoroughly.

The Shadow's professional attitude was useful. It reduced the risk of Bolan's having to shoot it out with his partner before the job was done.

The third day was another bloodless job, sinking a fishing boat the Capezzis used for their drug operations. The only man in sight when the two soldiers appeared was the boat keeper, a Portuguese fisherman who must have been close to eighty.

Bolan rendered him unconscious quietly, with an arm laid gently across his throat, then bound him lightly. While the Shadow torched the boat, the Executioner stuffed five hundred dollars into the man's pockets. Then he arranged the ropes so that even the old man's strength would be enough to get out of them in a few minutes.

"You really are a soft touch," the Shadow commented after they'd seen the boat on fire from end to end.

"Going to start on that again?"

"No, but would a Tong soldier have done that?"

"No, but why not make Don Marco wonder if somebody else has joined in? Besides, that boat-keeper job was probably all the old guy had in the world. At least I gave him enough to buy a bus ticket down to wherever his kids live.''

''It's your money.''

Actually it was Hal Brognola's. Bolan would rather have used the money from the bookmaker's, but the bills might be marked. If anyone found the old man with them on him, he'd be in trouble with more people than the Capezzis. Money from the Stoney Man ''contingency fund'' was safely anonymous.

They put sixty miles between them and the boat before noon, then found a neighborhood Italian restaurant. Over the antipasto, the Shadow suggested their next hit.

''This one's not going to be so easy. It's, well, we call it Don Marco's pleasure pit.''

''His private stock?''

''He has first crack, if you'll pardon the expression. But he uses it for paying favors. He also uses it for punishing any of the regular girls who step out of line, and breaking in the new ones.''

''New ones? Children?'' Bolan's voice was level, but the Shadow pushed himself back from the table by sheer reflex. Then he looked at the frozen mask Bolan's face had become.

''You into chickens?'' Incredibly the Shadow looked ready to draw.

''Do I look sick?''

''Not so's I've noticed, but then a lot of chicken pluckers don't.'' The Shadow shrugged. ''I don't pay for it much, anyway, and what can a kid give you?''

"I've never been interested in finding out, to tell the truth."

"Glad we agree on that," the Shadow said. "I wouldn't want you slow on the trigger when we hit Sally's."

"A hard target?"

"Average would be one Capezzi soldier, one guest with a bodyguard and Sally herself. She looks like a cross between Godzilla and the Wicked Witch from *Snow White*. She *would* run a chicken ranch if Don Marco gave her half a chance."

"Sounds like she's overdue for retirement."

The wine arrived, and the Shadow poured two glasses. "Let's drink to Sally's retirement, then."

Bolan sipped. There were some causes a man could drink to, even when he was drinking with a Mafia soldier.

11

Sally's "pleasure pit" was just outside Port Angeles, the old lumber port on the Juan de Fuca Strait. It was the same age as the Capezzi hideout where Bolan and the Shadow met, but not nearly as impressive. A lumber baron had built the first house. A lumberjack might have built the one the two men now approached.

The Shadow had said the place's security depended more on secrecy and an occasional bribe to the right policeman than on firepower, yet the two men parked a mile away and closed under cover of a misty dawn. For the last few hundred yards they used the cover of a weed-grown abandoned lot.

When they reached a garden loaded with more weeds and a few rotting cabbages, they stopped and checked their weapons.

"No point in splitting up," Bolan said, "unless we have to have prisoners."

"Nice but not necessary. But what about reinforcements?" The Shadow pointed. A Cadillac, a Camaro and what looked like the Buick used for the snatch on Bolan were parked in the driveway.

The warrior slipped a blackjack out of his sleeve, then patted his rucksack. "We can take out anybody in the cars first, then lay a charge on each car. Time the fuses for when we hit the house. I haven't met too many people who could cope with that much confusion."

"I hadn't met any until I met you," the Shadow replied. He sounded sincere. Bolan suspected he was also trying to flatter his partner into revealing more of his past.

From the foot of the driveway, they counted the men in the cars. Bolan saw one, apparently asleep, at the wheel of the Cadillac. Another walked back and forth between the Buick and the garage, puffing on a stogie. He had one piece on his hip and another in a shoulder holster.

The Shadow nodded and began to shift to the left, where he could cover both men and the door with his Browning. Bolan waited until the other was in position, then crawled along the fence, keeping well inside the long grass.

He reached the head of the driveway just as the walking hardguy decided to contemplate the scenery. He stood looking out over the fields for so long that Bolan wondered if he was going to have to use the Beretta.

Finally, when the man started to turn, Bolan uncoiled from his hiding place. One sinewy arm cut off the man's wind before he could even think of shouting. A muscular hand rapped the blackjack hard against the man's temple. He sagged, then slid out of Bolan's arms onto the gravel.

The slight noise was enough to wake the sleeping Cadillac driver. He hurled himself out of the vehicle, drawing a snub-nosed Colt Chief's Special as he did. A fast reaction, but not fast enough when the Shadow was waiting with a silenced Hi-Power.

Three 9 mm tumblers punched into the driver's head and chest. He stumbled back into the open door and sprawled on his back across the seat.

The Shadow had already retrieved the Chief's Special when Bolan tossed the fused charge in through the passenger window. Two charges went under the other two cars, and the soldiers headed for the cover of a dying birch tree halfway to the gate.

They'd just reached it when the front door opened and two men charged across the threshold. They clearly knew there was danger, but not from where. One gunner offered the Shadow a shot he couldn't resist.

Two 9 mm rounds slammed into the first man's chest. The second hardguy took cover behind the Buick. Bolan looked at his watch. Twenty seconds to go, ten—a shot from the Beretta kept the man in place—five, four, three, two, one—

The charge went off, flames and smoke erupting from under the Buick. The car leaped into the air, came down on its front wheels, tottered, then with horrible deliberation fell upside down on top of the gunner. If anybody in the house still wasn't alert, Bolan knew that the man's dying scream would finish the job.

Moments later the other two charges went off. The two gas tanks exploded with a boom that must have been heard for miles. The glass in all the windows and some of the shingles on the roof took off. More screams, women this time, echoed from inside the house. Bolan and the Shadow felt fragments sting exposed skin and patter down all around them. Bolan only hoped they wouldn't feel the fiery lick of burning gasoline.

As silence returned, except for the crackling of flames, the Shadow pointed at the door. "I'll make the first rush. You cover. But be careful. There has to be more firepower than usual in there."

"A VIP paying a call?"

"I won't complain if there is." The Shadow's muscular legs hurled him toward the house and up the stairs. As he crashed through the sagging door, splinters were gouged from the wood beside his head. The Hi-Power cracked twice, and a man toppled to the floor.

At the same time, somebody peered out a second-floor window. He saw Bolan, but instead of shooting he grabbed for something. It was a woman, hardly more than a teenager, with a bruised and bloody face. The hardguy cursed as he struggled to pull her around to use as a shield.

He'd underestimated both Bolan's speed and marksmanship. The Desert Eagle was in the Executioner's hands before the hardguy had his shield ready. But the only safe target was the man's head. The big pistol bucked twice. Two .44s decapitated the gunner as thoroughly as a guillotine, if not as neatly.

The woman fell back into the room with a shriek that told Bolan she was probably all right. But he wanted to make sure, and the porch roof was in reach of the window. One leap took him up onto the roof, a second took him in through the window.

Glass crunched under Bolan's weight as he landed. He bounced to his feet, glanced at the live woman and the dead gunner, then whirled as another woman's scream filled the room.

Two struggling figures fell out of a closet. One was a man, wearing only an undershirt and a shoulder holster. An S&W 25-5 filled his hand. The other was a woman, wearing nothing at all except a look of grim determination. She was clutching the man's gun hand with both of hers, and he was trying to swing around to beat her loose.

Bolan waited just long enough to pump a round into the man's chest to end the fight. The guy flew backward into the closet, hit the wall and slid down to sit on the floor with his eyes closed. Blood ran down the cracked lemon-colored plaster, more pooling on the closet floor.

"Take care—" Bolan said just as a shotgun roared from the hallway. Plaster crackled and crunched, a body crashed hard against something solid, then both a man and a woman were cursing furiously.

Out in the hall Bolan found the Shadow trying to bring his Hi-Power to bear and keep an Amazonian woman from doing the same with a shotgun. The Executioner closed in on the pair and chopped the woman smartly across the wrist. He caught the shotgun before it hit the ground, reversed it and held the weapon at hip level. The woman noticed that both barrels were pointed at her stomach and decided to stop struggling.

"Okay. Enough, I guess," she growled. She was fifty-something and must have looked unpleasant even when she was in a good mood.

"More than enough, if you're Sally," Bolan said. He broke the shotgun. "This is notice that you're out of business."

"Let me get my—"

The Shadow slapped her across one cheek with the barrel of the Hi-Power. It left only a red mark, but Bolan could see that the Shadow had pulled the blow.

"You get out of here right now with what you've got on." Which was a shocking purple dressing gown that had seen better days, somewhere around the time of the Korean War. If Sally wore anything under it, Bolan neither knew nor cared.

"You can't—" Sally began.

"I can send you out bare-ass, if you mouth off again," the Shadow snarled.

"She'd attract too much attention," Bolan said. He drew the Beretta and flipped off the safety. The metallic warning made Sally's face turn doughy-pale under the rouge and bruises.

"In two minutes you're out of here or you're dead meat," the Shadow threatened softly. Sally scampered down the stairs faster than Bolan would have expected from someone her size.

He shoved a fresh magazine into the Beretta. "We're going to have to rehearse the hard-soft act a little bit, Leon—" Then he noticed that the Shadow wasn't listening, but was staring at the dead man in the closet.

Bolan looked, too, and his eyebrows went up. The dead man was Antonio Pescaglia, the Capezzi's chief soldier. A VIP indeed—and a really big hole blown in the Capezzis' strength.

"I think it's Pescaglia, too, if you want my opinion," Bolan said. "But I think we ought to clear the house first, just in case Sally's decided to phone for help."

The Shadow shook himself like a man suddenly waking up from a deep sleep with an absorbing dream. He turned, and his face showed a mixture of relief, triumph, doubt and other feelings Bolan couldn't identify.

"Okay. But one of us ought to stay with the girls. There should be a third one—"

"Hi," a voice said in the doorway. Bolan had the Beretta raised before he saw that the woman's sheer nightgown couldn't have concealed a weapon. It certainly didn't conceal anything else. She was a real redhead with a rather hard face but an excellent figure.

"Hi, Gloria," the Shadow replied. "You coming with us, or going with Sally? One, two, three—"

"With you, with you," Gloria said urgently. "Now, can I get my stuff?"

"I'll come with you," Bolan stated, "just in case there's somebody holding out. Get the first-aid kit, too."

Houses like this, he knew, frequently had better first-aid kits than some ambulance services. It helped to be able to patch up the women without calling a doctor, if one of the customers got a little rough.

"Follow me," Gloria directed.

Bolan stayed three feet behind the woman, gun in hand, as they walked down the hall to her room. Gloria was clearly a good ten years older than the other two women, and probably a volunteer for this house. But if she wanted to unvolunteer, Bolan wasn't going to stop her.

"Can I pack a suitcase?"

"After we deliver the first-aid kit."

"It's under the sink in the john."

Bolan didn't need to move to keep an eye on Gloria as she pulled plastic bags out from under the bathroom sink. She'd just gathered them up when movement outside caught the Executioner's attention. He crouched, then moved to the window.

"What's—"

"Down, now!"

Gloria hit the floor. "Is it Sally or—"

Bolan put a finger to his lips and studied the running figure. It was a man, heading away from the house as fast as he could without making an easy target of himself. He'd rush from one hiding place to another, wait for reaction from the house, then continue on.

On the guy's last run Bolan saw that he was a young man, tall, muscular, with short blond hair. He wore a short-sleeved shirt, jeans and a shoulder holster. His right arm bore a multicolored tattoo, a long string of something Bolan couldn't make out at this distance. But they might have been hot-air balloons.

Corporal Goss. The runaway Marine had been here and armed, but instead of fighting was running away. That could mean a lot of things, but the only way to find out which was to chase him down.

Not an easy job, with a fit man who had a head start and didn't want to be caught. More than likely not a good idea, either, if it meant leaving the Shadow and Gloria behind. Bolan didn't entirely trust them with the two younger women. He certainly didn't trust them not to lay their hands on all the evidence and portable property in the house.

"Who was it?" Gloria asked.

"Couldn't see," Bolan replied shortly.

Without a word Gloria pulled her nightgown over her head and started jerking on underwear. A minute later she was completely dressed.

Not wanting to let the woman out of his sight, Bolan took her with him as he searched the upper floor of the house. It held little evidence and no surprises—not even the soundproof room with the handcuffs, whips and exotic leather underwear. The Capezzis had a bad reputation as far as "breaking in" new girls went, entirely apart from the late-and-unlamented Garrado brothers.

"No sign of any holdouts?" the Shadow asked when they'd joined him downstairs. He'd finished bandaging the feet of the new girl, whose name turned out to be Kathy. With bandages on her worst injuries and a housedress covering the others, she didn't look quite so much like the victim of a freeway head-on.

Bolan shook his head. "Spotted somebody running off, but he was too far away. We'll be out of here before he gets his nerve back. Any sign of Sally?"

"Like the guy you saw, I think she's still running." The Shadow leathered his Hi-Power and stood. "Only problem now is that Kathy can't walk. Should I get the car or should we try carrying her?"

It might save time, bringing the car up to the house from its hiding place a mile away, but the Shadow would be out of Bolan's sight for quite a while, with both Goss and Sally still unaccounted for. The warrior turned a mental thumbs-down on the risk, and started thinking of a tactful way to say it.

The distant wail of a siren settled the matter. "I guess we have to get clear first and worry about the car later," the Shadow said. He reached into the rucksack he'd dropped on the couch and pulled out one of the bombs. A twist of the wrist set the fuse, and a jerk with the other hand opened the basement door. The bomb bounced down into the darkness.

"Hey—" Gloria began.

"You want to leave all kinds of evidence for the cops?" the Shadow asked. "You can always go down and put out the fire if you really want to."

The woman laughed harshly. "Sorry. It's just that Sally's got a megabuck stash somewhere around the place. I was thinking she might have gone down there to fish it out. If she hadn't, maybe we could."

"Right," Bolan said. "And ten minutes later the police arrive and find us holding twenty years' worth of the stuff."

"He's right," the Shadow agreed. "Let's move it."

With the two men taking turns carrying Kathy, the party was out of the house before the bomb went off. Half the house collapsed, and a raging fire was out of control before the first police cruiser pulled up.

12

"So nobody's going to learn much about the hit?" Brognola asked when Bolan finished his story.

"I doubt it. That fire's going to leave it another unsolved incident in the war. If anybody gets suspicious, we'll both hear about it from Al Torstensson. I'm not going to lose sleep until then."

"Don't lose sleep over Sally, either," Brognola told him. "The police pulled her in. If we can get the girls to testify, she might not be out for a long time. She's been running this sort of operation for different gangs for years."

"I wouldn't recommend squeezing the girls. The younger two would like to go home or at least make a new start. Gloria may want to stay in the life. They'll all be in trouble if they wind up on the hit list of Sally's friends."

"I didn't know the old woman had any," Brognola said.

"Maybe not friends. More like people she knows too much about."

In the ensuing silence Bolan sensed Brognola's frustration.

"Besides," he added, "Don Pietro takes the old Mafia vow of silence fairly seriously."

"After hiring you?" Brognola sounded incredulous.

"He and the Shadow only tell me as much as I need to know for a particular mission. That's more than we could learn otherwise, but they keep quiet about everything else."

"Including Corporal Goss?"

"I've asked. They haven't answered."

Bolan heard the Justice Department man sigh. "It probably won't matter if they do. Goss may be out of our hands now."

"Who found him?"

"A state trooper, outside of Olympia. Goss was in a stolen car. The trooper pulled him down, and Goss went for a gun."

"Then what happened?"

"That's the weird part. Goss decked the trooper, then ripped out his radio and slashed his tires. He was packing a .45 but didn't even try to draw it. The trooper's got a sore jaw and a wounded ego, but nothing else."

Bolan's instincts painted the picture for him in vivid colors. "Hal, make sure the details don't get out. I don't care who you have to call or bribe, but make sure the Capezzis don't hear that Goss pulled his punches."

"The trooper wouldn't say that."

"The trooper might not be saying anything at all if he'd run into your average Mafia recruit who was trying to make his bones. I'd bet you anything the Capezzis are squeezing Goss to make his bones so there's no going back. He's fighting them. If they know how hard, he's dead meat.''

"Okay, okay," Brognola replied. "I'll do what I can. You do what you can about the three girls. Maybe we can't get Sally, and Pescaglia's gone, but there's got to be *something* they know.''

"I'm sure there is, but I'm going to take my time learning it.''

"Oh? That's not like you, Mack.''

"It is when the girls are guests of Donna Westin.''

"Donna— Oh.''

"Right. She's a family-law specialist, so she's got the right contacts. But she's also Don Pietro's second daughter.''

"Why the hell did you let her take them?''

"It wasn't a question of 'let,' '' the Executioner replied. "It was a question of finding out where they'd gone after they were already there.''

DON ETTORE MANGNANI reminded Don Marco Capezzi of an elderly crane. He was tall, stooped and long nosed. He wasn't, unfortunately, birdbrained, as well.

"You make a great many conditions for someone in your position,'' Mangnani observed. His tone was mild, but Capezzi was watching the man's eyes.

"My position is stronger than yours, and always will be.'' It was a childish speech, but Don Ettore had unsettled him more than he'd realized.

"I haven't lost a dozen men and four operations in the past week. I haven't lost my best soldier, or indeed any good soldiers at all.''

"That will change soon enough."

"Oh? I thought only those Don Pietro Brito saw as enemies were in danger."

The Don choked down outrage. Was Mangnani really saying that he would stand by and let that old fool throw ten million dollars to three *women?* To see money that could buy an army go to purchase perfume and underwear, if they weren't the shameless modern kind of woman who wore none?

He made a low noise in his throat. Threats wouldn't move Don Ettore. He should have realized that from the first. A threat made by a man who had no means to carry it out had always been a waste of breath.

Capezzi decided that he, too, was growing old, or he wouldn't have forgotten such a thing that he'd learned before he was twenty. But old as he was, he was going to outlive Don Pietro Brito and have the man's money in the bargain!

It was time to play his best card.

"If it was only Don Pietro's foolishness we faced, I wouldn't quarrel with you. I wouldn't like to see you standing aside, but I wouldn't make an issue of it.

"However, more important matters are at stake. We face a man who may make more than an issue of this fight if we don't work together. He may make this fight the end of us all in the Northwest. Do you want to see all our territory and money, not just Don Pietro's, going to the Chinese?"

"I won't live to see that, whatever Don Pietro does," Don Ettore pointed out. "But I admit that if there is that danger—"

Don Marco pulled out the file Pescaglia had so painstakingly assembled. It was a worthy monument to a man who had been the Don's right arm for ten years. It should also be convincing to Don Ettore.

It was. In five minutes the other Don's face had turned pale, and he seemed to have difficulty breathing. Don Marco wondered if the man was going to have a heart attack on the spot.

"Traitor!" Don Ettore finally gasped.

"Yes, he certainly is for employing the Executioner. It goes against our laws, our customs and common sense."

"I think the two of us together have more than common sense to pit against the Executioner," Don Ettore replied. "Shall we discuss that?"

The next ten minutes of talk covered more ground than the two Dons had gone over in the previous hour. It was also much more pleasant for Don Marco.

"But no attacks on Brito relatives, please," Don Ettore concluded. "I don't say that you're planning any. I don't even say that you carried out any. Yet one hears rumors. What one man may hear, others in New York may also hear. New York, and elsewhere."

What Don Marco thought about the Commission wasn't something he wanted Don Ettore to hear. It would give the other man information to sell to men who might bid high for it. So he spoke more mildly then he felt.

"Sam Brito had offended other people besides me, and more seriously. I don't say I felt friendship toward him, but I didn't think he was a great enemy."

"Good. Then our alliance seems to be settled. Shall we drink upon that?"

As he poured out wine, Don Marco considered that the situation was indeed good, better than Don Ettore knew—although perhaps not for Don Ettore. The other Don was indeed old. The Mangnanis would need a new capo soon, even if they became part of the Capezzi Family.

Don Ettore's chief soldier, Lucco Contamine, was almost as good as the late Antonio Pescaglia. With a little more seasoning, he'd be as good or better. He didn't have some of Don Marco's tastes, but he was no weakling in spite of this.

For a chance to be capo of the Mangnanis and share in everything that went with that honor, Contamine might sell his own daughter. He'd certainly not balk at dealing with somebody else's daughter.

And meanwhile, he could "make his bones" for Don Marco by dealing with Corporal Goss. The Marine, Capezzi suspected, would soon be useless as a link to the Silent Brotherhood. He'd never had any other use, so it would soon be time for him to go.

BOLAN WAS SITTING with his back to the wall and a map spread on the coffee table when someone knocked. He drew the Beretta and folded the map.

"My wife wants to talk to you about opening a sewing shop," the knocker said, uttering an arranged code.

"Come on in, Monty," Bolan replied. The door opened, and two hundred thirty pounds of ex-Air Policeman filled the doorway.

Pelham sat down. "Got a beer?"

"In the kitchenette."

Pelham came back with two Coors. Bolan waved his aside.

"How's Al?"

Bolan hadn't heard from Al Torstensson for a couple of days. He wasn't worried, but he needed to know about all his friends and allies now. Things were likely to start happening fast, now that he'd taken out the Capezzis' chief soldier.

"The boss says his arm'll be out of the sling in a couple days. He also says *his* bosses'll be out of his hair for a while, as long as he doesn't get into any more shoot-outs."

"So that means he won't be in the field with us?"

"No way. You're looking at the field man. But the boss says he may be able to sweet-talk a chopper out of the service department."

"What about a safe pilot?"

"You're looking at him, too. I'm current in Jet Rangers and Hueys."

"Do you mind my asking why you're not in a flying job?"

"I was, up to three years ago. That's when things started going bad, between me and the old lady. I figured if I was home more, it'd be better for her and the kids. I guess her mind was already made up, though."

"Okay." A helicopter would be invaluable for surprise attacks against a Capezzi Family that now must be fully alert. It would also make wild leaps into the dark a lot easier, but Bolan relied on good Intelligence and common sense to cut that risk.

Bolan unfolded the map. Pelham whistled at all the red marks. "That looks like a map of the gang war they've been talking about."

"It is. The hits already made, and a few we're planning."

"So let's go waste a few mafiosi."

"Monty, there's one thing I didn't tell you the first time around. Some of the mafiosi are on our side."

"Run that one past me again?"

Bolan did. Pelham finally stopped shaking his head and grinned.

"My father always told me to stay away from the gangs. He'll get a laugh out of where I've been, if I can ever tell him. Right now he thinks it's somebody I pissed off in the Air Force who wants a piece of my hide."

"You needed to tell him anything?"

"Had to tell him something when I dumped the kids on him. My mother-in-law's okay, but she's right here in town and an old lady. My dad's all the way out in Spokane, and he once faced down three Ku Kluxers. Besides, the mother-in-law might tell my ex, and I've heard that lady's started hitting the bottle. No telling what she might say and where."

Bolan nodded. He was beginning to like Pelham, and feel comfortable having the man at his back. He might not be as experienced as Al Torstensson, but he was available. He also might not be as deadly as the Shadow, but that was a point in his favor.

The more the Executioner learned about the Shadow, the more he seemed to be very much like Don Pietro Brito. He was a man who could have fought, and fought well, for any cause he chose. Then he chose to fight for the Mafia.

GLORIA LOOKED OUT the back window of the Westin house. The back lawn was narrow and sloped up sharply, ending in an even steeper hillside that was thick with second-growth pine and a dozen kinds of bushes, vines and ground cover.

It made sense to keep out of the backyard. An army could hide there, not just a sniper. But she couldn't go out in the front yard, either. Not without making the neighbors talk, or so Mrs. Westin said.

Even if the neighbors didn't talk, the two men watching the house would. Gloria knew who they had to be, and didn't want to give them the chance to say even a single word.

No backyard. No front yard. No anywhere outside the house without one of the Westins and usually one of the soldiers along. No going into the kids' wing of the house—a whole wing of a house this size, for just two kids!

Gloria remembered her own childhood, where four kids were packed into an apartment about the size of the Westins' living room. Her dad being drunk most of the time made it seem even smaller. Most of the time when he got drunk he hit the kids, or did even worse with the girls, and that didn't help, either.

By the time Gloria was sixteen, the apartment had shrunk down to the size of a coffin. Which was exactly what it would have been if she hadn't got out.

She did get out, and the past ten years could have been a lot worse. She suspected it was time to make a break, but she'd be damned if she was going to sit around on her tail and wait for Donna Westin to do it all nice and legal.

For one thing the law moved slowly. For another thing Gloria wanted out of Seattle. There was a man who could move fast, but she had to get to him first.

She went into the kitchen, where Kathy, one of the two other girls from Sally's, was hobbling back and forth between the stove and the breakfast nook. It looked as if Donna's kids were on their third helping of pancakes.

"Hey, don't you have to be off to school pretty soon?" Gloria asked.

The older child, Rick, shook his head. "Naw. We got the rest of the week off. Teachers' conference, or something like that."

Gloria's nerves tingled. If her friend was going to help her, he'd have to hustle. Donna Westin was at the office most of the day. Her husband was in New York, meeting editors. The housekeeper and the two other girls were all grown-ups; they could run.

But the kids—she didn't want her friend to meet them if she could help it. She trusted him a long way, but not that far.

At least she had to start somewhere. She picked up the phone and dialed.

"Hello, this is Morning Glory. Can I leave a message for Spider? No? Well, I'll call back later today, then. Thanks."

"Who's Speeder?" Donna's other child, Fiona, asked.

"Spider, like in Spiderman," Gloria said. "He's an old friend. I think he might lend me a little money for some new clothes, so I can go job hunting."

Kathy's eyes met hers over the heads of the kids. Then she nodded.

Good. She wouldn't talk. Just as well. Donna Westin had to know her way around a bedroom—or if not, then she was wasted on that hunk of a husband. But she might not like her kids knowing how Cousin Gloria was going to get out of Seattle.

Lucco Contamine, the Spider, was generous to women, but they had to be generous to him first.

13

"Come on, Gloria, it's been a long day," Donna Westin complained. "I need the shower."

Gloria decided she really didn't need to wash her hair again. She could shift to the guest bathroom and finish there, but Lucco might show up any minute. She didn't want him to catch her in the shower, not until they'd had a chance to bargain a little.

She also didn't want Donna Westin meeting the man at the door. Somehow Gloria had the feeling that the straight-arrow Mrs. Westin knew a little more than she let on about her father's "business connections."

Gloria turned off the shower, wrapped a towel around herself and stepped out of the bathroom. Donna Westin came in, pulling off her jacket as she did. Gloria started down the hall to the back bedroom. After a minute she heard the water running again.

She stopped by a hall window that gave her a view of the street. A taxi stopped and two men got out. One of them wore a turtleneck sweater and jeans, the other a blazer and black slacks.

Good. One of the men had to be Lucco, and she'd be able to meet him at the door. Maybe not wearing as much as she'd like, but of course that wouldn't make any difference in the long run....

The two men turned toward the house, and Gloria had to grip the windowsill to keep from falling. One of the men *was* Lucco Contamine. The man with him was someone she knew only as "the Boot," but would never forget. He and Antonio Pescaglia had had the pleasure of her company one night, and it was three weeks before the bruises were gone.

The Boot had also been number-two soldier to Don Marco Capezzi.

Analysis had never been Gloria's strong point, and anyway, the situation didn't need any. She had one thought: the kids.

Clutching the towel about her, she dashed to the kitchen. As she ran, she prayed that Lucco would take a minute or two to case the house before moving in.

"Thank God!"

Kathy was in the kitchen, pouring herself a glass of milk. She stared at Gloria as the older woman rushed forward.

"Where are the kids?"

"In the playroom with Sheila."

"Thank God!"

"What's all this thanking God?"

"Some soldiers from the Capezzis— I saw them outside. Go downstairs fast, get Sheila and the kids and get them out the French doors. If you get into the woods before the Capezzis arrive—"

Kathy turned so pale that for a moment Gloria thought the girl was going to faint. Then she nodded and ran for the stairs. Gloria saw her bite her lip at the pain from her feet, but she kept going.

Absently Gloria picked up the glass of milk. She had a gut feeling that it would be a good idea to warn Mrs. Westin, too, but it would be impossible to hide that from the soldiers. They'd probably get Donna just the same, and what would happen to Gloria then...?

The milk turned to a lump of lead in her stomach. The doorbell rang. "See who it is, Gloria," came a voice from the bathroom.

Gloria had just reached the front door when three shots crackled outside. As she unlatched the door, it flew open, knocking her onto the hall rug and stripping the towel off her.

"On your feet, Gloria," Contamine demanded. He didn't take his eyes off her as she stood, didn't help her with the towel or even point his gun away. "Where's Donna Westin?"

"In the shower."

The Boot chuckled. "Come on." The two men vanished toward the rear of the house. From the way they moved, they obviously knew the layout. Gloria prayed that the girls and the kids were already outside.

Two more soldiers appeared in the doorway and took positions on either side of the front hall. Gloria recognized one of them. He'd been at Sally's for a couple of days, and she'd heard that he was a Marine deserter. He certainly looked like it; he was even hunkier than Mr. Westin. If he'd asked for her, she'd have given him at least a discount.

A scream burst from the back of the house. The two soldiers reappeared, dragging a nude-and-dripping Donna Westin.

"What the devil have you got us into, Gloria?" she snapped.

The Boot backhanded her across the face. She glared and looked ready to spit on him. Gloria hoped she wouldn't. The Boot might lose control then, and Mrs. Westin might lose a lot more.

Donna's face only twisted, and Contamine shifted position and got ready to draw. The Boot's hand fell to his side.

"If you don't mind, we'll ask the questions," Contamine said quietly. "Where are your children and the other girls from Sally's?"

"The housekeeper took them out shopping," Donna replied.

"And what about you?" the Boot asked with a look at Gloria she didn't like at all.

"In case Lucco didn't tell you," she answered, "we had a date. I wouldn't stand him up to ride herd on a couple of kids and a pair of hard-luck cases."

The two soldiers handcuffed Donna Westin, then used another pair of cuffs to hobble her ankles. They didn't bother offering her any clothing, but she seemed to be ready to wear her skin as if it came from Paris or Milan.

Gloria decided that Mrs. Westin was a cooler customer than she'd thought, and that something might come of this. Good for the women, bad for the Capezzis.

The two soldiers now started an argument in Sicilian. Gloria understood the dialect just well enough to follow most of the talk.

The Boot was saying that Mrs. Westin had to be lying, because they'd killed two Brito soldiers. If the housekeeper had gone off with the others, one or both of the soldiers would have gone with her.

Contamine was saying that the Boot had his brains in his ass if he had any at all. They couldn't be sure that Don Pietro had assigned only two soldiers to guard his daughter; it would make more sense for him to send four. So the two might be back, and if they saw anything suspicious they'd call up reinforcements. They had Donna Westin, who was their main goal; they didn't have time to argue about anything else.

They finally compromised on a quick search of the house. The Marine went out in back, and a second soldier went downstairs. Gloria prayed—as she hadn't since she was a girl—that neither of them would see anything.

"Nobody downstairs," the second soldier said.

Gloria swallowed.

The Marine appeared from the kitchen. "Nobody out back that I can see. It's a friggin' jungle out there, anyway."

Gloria wanted to sigh with relief, but the Marine was looking at her. She got the feeling he knew she recognized him, but was hoping she wouldn't talk. She decided that the Marine would get his wish.

As if she'd been removing the last garment in a strip act, Gloria took off her towel and handed it to Donna

Westin. "Here, Donna. I think you can get more out of this than I can."

Handcuffs and hobbles didn't help, but Donna Westin did manage to get the towel more or less around her. "What about her?" Contamine said, pointing at Gloria.

"I don't care if she's Miss America. The drivers keep their eyes on the road, or I have a little talk with them."

Gloria wanted to grin. The Boot had more faith in his soldiers' powers of concentration than she had. Even if they didn't do anything on the way, they'd be thinking of her as available....

A hand slammed into the small of her back. "Okay, you want to run around bare tailed? Then start running."

DON MARCO'S SMILE WIDENED as he listened to the Boot finish his report.

"Good. Very good. The Mangnanis cooperated fully? Even better. Where...? I think the houseboat, to start with. But be ready to move it. No, move it tonight. Wait for full dark and have the alternate site picked, but don't delay any longer... No, no. I gave orders, but the honor of this victory belongs to all of us. I must use the limbs of younger men, even if I can still use my own wits. When those younger men are as good as you are, old men like me can sleep in peace. Goodbye."

The Capezzi capo hung up and lit the one cigar a day he allowed himself. The affair hadn't gone perfectly, because the children had escaped. Having them as well would have put even more pressure on both Don Pietro and Mr. Westin.

It might also have meant a quarrel with Don Ettore. The old fool might think that even snatching Mrs. Westin broke the agreement about families. Certainly he'd have had something to say about the children.

Then there would have been a quarrel, and even perhaps the end of the alliance with the Mangnanis. That alliance promised more than all of Don Pietro's grandchildren put together!

After all, Don Pietro would surely yield now. Then there would be that ten million dollars in Don Marco's hands. With the Mangnani soldiers added to the Capezzis, the money would do much more good.

There was also Gloria, who would make up for a good deal. She was dead, but she didn't know it yet. Before she learned the fact, she'd give much pleasure. After she learned, she'd give even more pleasure of another kind in dying.

DONNA WESTIN'S strained voice faded, and nothing but the hiss of the tape and a faint rippling sound filled the greenhouse. In his lounge chair Don Pietro seemed to have stopped breathing. The Shadow stood behind the chair, looking more like his nickname than usual.

"Don Pietro," the Executioner said, "I'd like to have that tape analyzed."

The Shadow shook his head, but Don Pietro straightened up. "Who'd do the analysis?"

"Friends of mine."

"Friends you trust?"

"Absolutely. I'd trust them with my life."

"That is honorable. But would these friends be so honorable where the Families are concerned?"

"I'd ask them to be." Bolan was going to keep that promise if Don Pietro let him have the tape.

"But they might not do what you ask, is that it? Because they serve other masters, or at least have divided loyalties?"

Bolan didn't like either Don Pietro's line of argument or the way the Shadow was looking at him. He decided to retreat gracefully.

"I couldn't promise absolute discretion."

"Then the tape must remain in our hands. Nothing less than complete silence will be enough. When we have my daughter back, and her children can play soccer with Don Marco's head—" The hard old face twisted in a spasm of rage.

"I understand." That was the truth. It was also true that Bolan's understanding wouldn't delay Don Pietro's death by one second once they'd settled with Don Marco.

The Brito capo had a father's concern for his daughter. That was fine. It would have been even finer if somewhere along the line he had developed an equal concern for other people's children. Preferably, Bolan thought, before he'd brought danger, grief, suffering and death to so many of them.

Don Pietro had long since burned his bridges behind him. Donna Westin was an entirely different situation.

"Don Pietro," Bolan said, "how much danger do you want your daughter to face?"

The Shadow frowned, but Don Pietro held up a hand. "No. All that Mr. Belasko has done for us has earned him the right to speak as frankly as you. I hope I don't need to say this again."

"No, Don Pietro," the Shadow said. Bolan heard an unusual note in the man's voice, but couldn't quite put a name on it. His instinct that there was some connection between the Shadow and the capo flared up again.

"Now, I'd like to say 'none.' But even if I sent you out tonight with the ten million in cash, my daughter would have twenty-four hours at the mercy of Don Marco. That's like being at the mercy of the Devil.

"So I think we can't hurt Donna if we do a little searching. I'll make the money ready, so we can meet Don Marco's deadline if there's no choice. But I'll also listen to any ideas you may have about how to give ourselves choices."

"I'd like to let Mr. Fieromosca go first," Bolan said. "Without revealing any Family secrets, he may know some things that I don't."

The Shadow nodded slowly.

"We've got to keep in mind one thing first, last and foremost. Where Donna is, the Capezzis and the Mangnanis are going to have a whole lot of soldiers. If we have to fight our way in, it'll take long enough for them to kill her. Even if we beat them down before that, there'll be all kinds of stray bullets flying around."

"So you say we should be subtle rather than coming in force?" Don Pietro asked.

The Shadow grinned. "We Sicilians are supposed to be good at being sneaky. Just because Don Marco's about as sneaky as a drunken elephant doesn't mean we have to do it his way."

"Indeed, no," Don Pietro said. "I suppose our being subtle depends somewhat on Mr. Belasko's cooperation."

Bolan decided to take that as a question. "Don Pietro, it doesn't matter that you didn't want to trust some of my friends with your secrets. That's between you and your conscience. What lies between us is nothing that will keep me from doing my best to see your daughter alive and free."

Again Bolan's words would have passed a lie-detector test. The Shadow was absolutely right about their finding Donna Westin surrounded by Capezzi and Mangnani soldiers. Quite unintentionally the Don's daughter had served as bait for her father's enemies.

Now, if her father's friends could just kill the sharks before they ate the bait . . .

"Another thing," the Shadow went on. "We owe Gloria one. If she hadn't warned Kathy, Don Marco might have the whole kit and caboodle."

"Then Don Marco would have his money," Don Pietro said, nodding. "You have a point. We won't save Gloria at the cost of my daughter. But if we can save both, Gloria will have my protection, as much as she needs."

"Excuse me, Don Pietro," Bolan said, "but if she now wants to start over, she might want another protector. I can arrange one. And since she knows none of your secrets, only those of the Capezzis—''

"Of course. Let it be as she wishes," the Don said with a courtly wave of a thin hand. "But she'll have my gratitude and some money at the least."

"Let's not count our chickens before they hatch," the Shadow advised. "If we're going to move in fast, that means we need to know where they are. I think that lapping sound in the background is water. My guess is, they're on the houseboat."

Don Pietro nodded. Bolan tried not to look blank.

"Sorry. We gave you everything that was on the target list, but that houseboat wasn't, until now." The Shadow marked a location in Dabob Bay. "It's a converted lumber barge, really, not one of those floating fiberglass bungalows. They could have ten, twenty soldiers aboard."

"How do they move it?"

"Slowly and carefully, unless the weather's good."

Bolan nodded. "Then if you do not mind my calling another of my friends . . ."

"Will *this* one at least hold his tongue?" Don Pietro asked. His mask of calmness seemed to be slipping.

"Yes. I know how to keep him silent. My word of honor."

More truthful lying. Monty Pelham would certainly keep his mouth shut, because he'd know that Bolan would tell his boss if he didn't. Al Torstensson wouldn't be happy about slipups that put anybody's children in danger, even a Mafia Don's.

"Then I think I can have a helicopter ready to search, tomorrow morning."

"Bless you," Don Pietro said. "I think any more planning can wait until we have the helicopter and some sleep. Mr. Belasko, if you wish to accept my hospitality for the night..."

"Thank you, but I need to pull some equipment together. I'll be here at dawn."

14

Bolan suspected that the Huey's career must have begun during the Vietnam War. From the way its engine sounded, that career might be about to end in Tarboo Creek.

Five miles south, at the mouth of the creek, lay the Capezzi houseboat. At this distance the helicopter wouldn't look suspicious, if anyone even saw it.

The Executioner lay on the floor and adjusted the focus on the telescope. The houseboat's image wavered with the vibration from the helicopter, but its identity was no longer in doubt. The Capezzis had moved it far enough to delay a ground search, but Bolan had always intended to take to the air.

He locked the camera to the eyepiece of the telescope, adjusted the focus again, then held the telescope in position while the shutter clicked four times. One good shot plus the maps and charts, and they'd have all they needed for planning.

"We going to be here much longer?" Monty Pelham shouted above the roar of the rotors. "This baby's a real pig for fuel."

They could set down for an emergency refueling at some other heliport, but that would mean delay and could threaten security. The Executioner gave the thumbs-up signal. Pelham returned it and swung the Huey into a turn. Bolan yanked the door shut and slid across the cabin.

"Are we really going to need both the chopper and the boat?" the Shadow asked.

"Not unless we can put some of Don Pietro's soldiers in place as land-side backup."

The Shadow frowned. "You sound like you don't trust my men."

"It doesn't matter what I trust or don't. Don Pietro gave us his orders. He sounded like he meant business."

The Shadow nodded. "I would, in his position."

Bolan checked the film magazine in the camera as the Huey climbed to cruising altitude and headed north.

"YOU MAY USE HER UP, of course," Don Marco said, answering the Boot's unspoken question. "As long as she makes enough noise, it doesn't matter if she survives. Make sure that Goss takes part. A *full* part. He didn't make his bones by taking down two of Don Pietro's men. Not as I see it.

"How many men should you leave behind on the houseboat? If I need to answer that question, then perhaps I should become an honest man. I don't have enough good soldiers to make a living as a capo!"

No one who heard the tone of Don Marco Capezzi's voice as he spoke would have thought those last words a joke.

THE SILENCE THAT FOLLOWED the end of the tape seemed a living thing, reaching out claws toward Don Pietro. He looked at the big man in the other lounge chair under the plum tree.

"The bastards," Tom Westin said quietly.

Indignation flared in Don Pietro. "You take it very calmly."

"I take it calmly, Don Pietro, because that woman screaming wasn't Donna."

The capo's mouth fell open. Hope surged, replacing indignation. He forced himself to speak calmly.

"Why do you think so?"

"I've been married to Donna for eleven years. I have a trained ear for voices. I know what she sounds like under just about any kind of stress—"

"Including being tortured?"

Westin laughed. "If I even thought of trying that, your daughter would have my balls hanging in her office, as a warning to wife beaters. No. But I'll give you ninety-eight chances out of a hundred, that's Gloria, not Donna."

"I pray you are right." Don Pietro's heart was still fluttering in a way that he didn't like and his doctor would have liked even less. But it no longer felt as if it would stop abruptly.

"I think I am," Westin said. "There's another thing, too. I don't think Don Marco would undercut his negotiating position. The longer Donna stays in one piece, the better that position is."

"Again, I'll pray that you are right." Don Pietro thought his son-in-law probably was. Tom Westin wore thick glasses, but otherwise he was both tough and shrewd. He'd even been a faithful husband to Donna, although Don Pietro knew that such a man could have had most women for the asking. He deserved something for the advice he'd given tonight, advice that had calmed the fears of a nervous old man—a nervous old father.

"Whether you're right or not, you deserve a token of my gratitude. I—"

"If you're going to be grateful before we get Donna back, I want only one thing. I want to go with the Shadow and Mr. Belasko to bring her home."

Don Pietro stared. It wasn't only the request. It was the fact that Westin had interrupted him for the first time in twelve years. Always before, the writer had shown as much respect to his father-in-law as if he'd been a Sicilian.

Well, neither of them was at his best tonight. That was another debt Don Marco would pay with blood.

"You've never been in the service—" Don Pietro began.

"No," Westin replied almost defiantly, touching his glasses. "But you know how much I hike, swim and work out. You've seen me shoot. I won't be deadweight."

"You might be dead, and my daughter a widow."

"Yes, and I might wind up a widower without lifting a finger to save Donna. Do you want your grandchildren asking me about *that?*"

If Don Marco Capezzi had appeared before him in that moment, Don Pietro would have tried to strangle him with bare hands. Nothing less would have eased the rage that filled him.

"They've already gone on tonight's mission," Don Pietro said at last. "If this isn't the last one, I'll ask them to take you on the next."

"Thank you, *padróne*," Westin said. He even had the accent right.

Don Pietro watched his son-in-law go, then pulled the tape recorder toward him and began to record a message. He had to try three times before his voice stayed steady, but in the end he had it.

"To Don Marco Capezzi and Don Ettore Mangnani. Release my daughter Donna Westin within twenty-four hours, unharmed. Otherwise, none of you will be alive twenty-four hours after that."

He only wished he could see their faces when they listened to the tape.

BOLAN SWUNG ONTO the skid of the Huey, and from there into the cabin. He waved to Lieutenant Thanh, whose help Brognola had enlisted, standing on the flying bridge of the cruiser, and to the Shadow, crouching in the stern. A moment later the cruiser's white bow-wave died as Thanh throttled back the engines.

Now the cruiser would drift, five miles out in the bay from the houseboat. On radar it would look like any other pleasure craft or fishing boat, until Bolan signaled.

Then it would cover those five miles in ten minutes. The Tongs had paid good money for two oversize diesel engines; the cruiser was fast. Ten minutes should be plenty of time, considering that everyone on the houseboat was going to be too busy to watch radar screens.

As Monty Pelham put the helicopter into a climb, Bolan started pulling on a parachute over his black-suit and weapons.

The photographs and the maps both said the same thing. The only open space near the houseboat big enough for an LZ was a little *too* close. Helicopters were noisy.

But open space big enough for a noisy chopper was also big enough for an expert jumper coming down in a silent parachute. From three thousand feet the helicopter would be less audible, unlikely to trigger an alarm.

Surprise. They had to have it, and if they kept it right through the fight until the last hardman was dead, so much the better. But they certainly had to have it at the beginning, or Donna Westin was dead.

That was why Bolan was approaching from the land side. From that direction he might take out any reinforcements on the way to the boat. He'd certainly get between them and the boat for as long as necessary.

Pelham flew with one hand for a moment while holding the folded map in the other hand. "ETA six minutes, Mike."

"Ready when you are," Bolan said as he made a final adjustment to the Weatherby's sling.

"Four minutes."

Bolan was trusting the Shadow more tonight than he had before. There wasn't any choice, since Monty Pelham was the only chopper pilot they had. The Executioner was fairly sure that the Shadow could be trusted, too, at least until Donna Westin was safe.

Whatever hold the Shadow had over Don Pietro, messing up Donna's rescue would be a death sentence for him.

"Two minutes."

Bolan walked to the door, lurching slightly from the motion of the Huey.

"One minute."

He mentally crossed his fingers, hoping that Monty Pelham was a really good map reader, as well as chopper pilot. Being impaled on a fir tree wasn't how he wanted to die.

"Coming up, ten-nine-eight—"

At "three" the warrior braced himself in the door. At "one" he flung himself out into the damp northwestern night.

15

The camouflaged parachute collapsed neatly, right on top of Bolan. He wrestled himself free of the damp nylon, unhooked the harness and headed for cover.

From inside a stand of scrub pine he watched the clearing. He counted off two minutes on the illuminated dial of his watch, then pushed his chute under a bush and moved out.

There was a well-trodden path between the clearing and the shore. Bolan stayed safely to one side of the path, far enough to be hard to hear and see, close enough to detect major movements on the path. He kept the shoulder-stocked Beretta in hand, loaded and locked.

Ten minutes brought him to the shore, a hundred yards west of the houseboat. A look through the night sight showed him two sentries nearby, two more on deck. The shore itself showed tire tracks, which looked like those of a four-wheel-drive vehicle.

Right. It seemed a better-than-even chance that Don Marco had done what Bolan would have done in his situation. He'd turned the houseboat into a trap, then moved the bait somewhere else once he knew the trap was going to be sprung.

That was bad luck for Donna Westin. It was even worse luck for the Capezzi and Mangnani hardmen left behind. If any of them knew where Donna had gone, they were going to be asked. Probably rather forcibly, if Bolan knew the Shadow. The man would have his orders, and the only way to keep him from carrying them out would be to shoot him dead.

Whatever problems the Shadow might cause, it was time to call him. Bolan unhooked his radio, adjusted frequencies and spoke one word.

"Gossamer."

The reply came back. "Gauze." Before the Shadow went off the air, Bolan heard the rumble of diesels as Thanh opened throttles.

The warrior had unslung the Weatherby to use the night sight. Now he loaded the weapon and put six rounds in his pockets. He raised the rifle, checked for a target and fired.

The Weatherby blazed. The first heavy slug caught the man on deck near the bow. The second dropped the man amidships.

Two down, and those the ones closest to cover. One of the men on shore was looking around frantically. The other had hit the dirt, which meant that he was more alert and therefore more dangerous. Not knowing which direction the bullets came from, he hadn't hidden himself adequately. Bolan had to punch a bullet through a bush to hit the man, but he rolled out from behind cover, thrashed briefly, then lay still.

That put the last man into motion, and brought three more men up from below. Bolan dropped the running man as he reached the gangplank. He threw up his arms, fell, skidded and took the gangplank with him as he fell into the water.

Very early the Executioner learned that victory can hang on taking advantage of such bits of luck. He ducked under cover of the trees, then sprinted toward the boat. Branches lashed his face, roots leaped from the ground to catch his toes, but he pressed on. He knew the Weatherby's sight might be taking a beating, but he also thought long-range work was finished for the night.

At a good range for the Beretta, Bolan went to ground. Two of the men had taken cover, but one was trying to fish the gangplank out of the water. The Executioner fired a 3-round burst that punched the hardguy and the gangplank overboard.

A rumble and a billow of smoke issued from the houseboat's stern. The Capezzis had fired up the big slow-speed diesel and were going to head for the safety of open water. Or what they thought was the safety of open water.

Bolan's mind leaped ahead. He had maybe two minutes to get aboard the houseboat. If he didn't, and Donna Westin was on the vessel, she'd be at the mercy of the remaining hardmen. The cruiser would be vulnerable when it showed up, and *he* might have trouble if reinforcements showed up from inland.

The best solution was to get aboard. Now.

He moved from cover, firing 3-round bursts from the Beretta on the run. His intention was to keep the hardmen down and nervous. It would probably make them think they faced several opponents. That idea was guaranteed to work on their nerves.

He rammed a fresh magazine into the Beretta, then scooped two grenades from a pocket, pulled both pins and launched the bombs.

They were smoke grenades. Nothing with a major load of high explosives or shrapnel was safe to use where Donna Westin might get hit. Both went off, though, with resounding bangs before they spewed green-and-white smoke all over the houseboat.

Noise, surprise and then the all-enveloping smoke turned nervousness into fear. A few bullets whistled past Bolan as he charged the houseboat. Somebody below put the diesel in gear as he reached the water's edge, but they were a second too late.

The warrior jumped, his powerful legs hurling him across the widening gap. He landed rolling, then came up with the Beretta in hand. He shot one hardman in the back and another in the chest as the man started to turn.

That should leave only one man on deck, and how many more below? Somebody had to be on the engine controls, but they were probably rigged for one-man operation. Seven men would be a good share of what the two Families, now allied against Don Pietro, could afford to spare for a trap.

Seven men, and six of them now dead or dying. Don Marco had no conscience to answer to. But he might have to answer to his own soldiers, if they kept going up against enemies who ate them like popcorn.

Another, more distant rumble reached Bolan, rising above the houseboat's engine. At the same time he spotted movement on the bank.

The range was long for the Beretta, but he used it for one 3-round burst. Nobody shouted or screamed, but nobody fired back, either. The movement got a lot faster all at once, then stopped entirely.

The reinforcements had hit the dirt. Bolan shifted position and slipped a third load into the Weatherby. By the time he'd finished, bullets were snapping overhead and smashing into the weathered wood of the pilothouse and deck.

The men on shore were uniformly firing high, a common mistake at night. Or maybe they weren't sure if any of their friends were still alive and were just trying to keep Bolan's head down.

For the moment, at least, they were succeeding. Neither Bolan nor his one remaining on-deck opponent could move without drawing fire. That could give any men below time to sort themselves out, organize a counterattack—and most of all, kill Donna Westin if she was aboard.

As usual, the firefight was turning into two steps forward, one step back. Also as usual, there were some parts of it Bolan could do nothing about. Such as Donna Westin. So he had to do the best he could about everything else.

He found a rest for the Weatherby and sighted on the first man on the bank. One round took the man down and increased the fire from the shore. It didn't increase the fire's accuracy. The houseboat was well under way now, a moving target in both range and azimuth, and hard to either hit or hit from. Unless a man was a marksman like the Executioner.

Bolan demonstrated his marksmanship twice more before the houseboat began to turn. As it turned, it hid him from the shore and the men on the shore from his sights.

As the boat turned, the warrior also caught sight of the cabin cruiser moving slowly, parallel to the houseboat's course but five hundred yards offshore. What was the Shadow doing, or leaving undone?

The Executioner pulled out his radio and shifted to the frequency for Monty Pelham. If the Shadow had turned traitor, the chopper had to be alerted to stay clear, if nothing else. The Shadow was carrying his G-3, with night sights as good as Bolan's, and could knock the Huey out of the sky without working up a sweat.

The houseboat turned again. Bolan estimated its course by what he could see of the shore. The boat seemed to be turning almost at random, as if the steersman was erratic or the steering mechanism defective.

Then over the diesel rumble Bolan heard whispered commands.

"A little to port. No, that's too much. Yeah, that's better...."

The last surviving hardman on deck had kept his head. He was whispering instructions to the helmsman below.

The helmsman, and who else? Bolan rolled over and studied the relative positions of the cruiser and the houseboat. If somebody had a long-range automatic weapon and stuck it out the pilothouse window, and if the houseboat turned a little farther to port ...

Bolan's body completed the thought for him. Ignoring the survivor, he lunged for the pilothouse. As he thudded against it, the glass shattered and a long black barrel thrust out over the warrior's head.

It was aimed directly at the cabin cruiser. Bolan still had enough time to act. With one hand he grabbed the barrel and heaved downward, which brought him up to where he could throw a smoke grenade through the shattered window and into the pilothouse.

The grenade's detonation blew out most of the remaining glass in the pilothouse. The last few bits vanished when the Shadow opened up. Bolan looked at the cruiser and saw that it had closed to three hundred yards while his attention was elsewhere.

The Shadow was going to stay on the side of the good guys, at least for tonight. Bolan canceled plans for calling the helicopter. Instead he called the cruiser.

"We're out of range from the shore. Keep their heads down, and I'll see who's below."

"That's a roger," came Lieutenant Thanh's voice, and Bolan heard the Shadow laugh.

The pilothouse looked more like a slaughterhouse, with two dead men sprawled in their own blood, chopped down by bursts of 7.62 mm NATO. In fact, the assault rifle had ruined just about everything except the weapon the two men had been ready to use—an M-60 machine gun with a full belt.

Don Marco, Bolan decided, had been dealing with some fairly high-powered underground arms dealers. It was a good thing he'd grabbed the barrel of the M-60 before it could fire on the cruiser.

Bolan pushed the machine gun aside and called down the hatch from the pilothouse. "Attention, below. This is a representative of the Brito Family. You have two minutes to produce Donna Westin, alive and in one piece."

"What the hell can you do to us without hurting her?" some quick thinker shouted back. From the murmurs of agreement, Bolan guessed there were at least three more men below.

"Just use your imagination. I'm sure you'll realize we're not helpless. You are, though. If you harm a hair of her head, you go, and slowly. If you come out with your hands up and Mrs. Westin alive, you can get over the side and join your friends on shore."

"That goes for Dominic, too?"

"The man on deck?"

"Yeah."

Bolan looked aft. The man called Dominic was sitting against the low rear of the deckhouse. His face was so bullet chewed that none of his friends below would have recognized him. He must have caught an extra burst from the G-3.

"It won't matter to Dominic."

"Shit!"

"You're in it, not us," Bolan said. He looked at the cruiser, now a hundred yards away and closing fast. The Shadow stood on the bow, Hi-Power ready. Lieutenant Thanh waved from the flying bridge and turned the spotlight on the pilothouse.

"Okay. We're coming up."

"Donna Westin first."

"She's passed out."

"Hurt?"

"Just fainted, I think. Hey, Don Marco made it pretty clear what would happen if we messed around—"

"Without his orders, anyway."

Silence. Then, "Okay, ditch your pieces. We ain't going to get a better deal, I'm thinking."

Guns clattered and clunked on plank decks, and the first of the hardmen began to climb the ladder. A second followed, and then a third, with a blanket-wrapped figure in a fireman's carry.

The last man set his burden down on the deck as if it had been a basket of eggs.

"Okay?"

"Let's just make sure—" Bolan began.

He never finished. A heavy hand darted into a cuff and came up with a holdout gun. The Executioner wasn't in the best position to stop the draw, but his speed made up for that. His foot slammed the hardman's gun hand against the pilothouse wall.

The other two hardmen used Bolan's distraction to break for the open. They were climbing the railing when the Hi-Power spoke. Four bullets dropped one man over the side, the other back on the deck. The man on the deck started to scream.

The cruiser slid alongside, bumping as Lieutenant Thanh throttled back. Then the Shadow leaped onto the houseboat's deck. He reached the pilothouse just as Bolan had knocked the gunman into unconsciousness.

"What are you fooling around with that asshole for?" the Shadow snarled.

"Prisoner," Bolan said. "I have a bad feeling that we've been had." He knelt and pulled the blanket way from the wrapped figure on the deck.

"Give the man a cigar," the Shadow replied glumly.

It was Gloria. Her face was covered with cuts, bruises and cigarette burns. Bolan unwrapped more of the blanket and saw the Shadow wince.

The Garrados were dead, but some pretty good amateurs at the art of giving pain had worked Gloria over from head to foot. At first Bolan thought she was dead. Then he thought that she might want to be dead if she could see herself.

Then his experience with wounds told him two things. Gloria wasn't dead. She was deeply unconscious, a combination of shock and probably a heavy dose of morphine. She also looked bad, but would almost certainly pull through if she got help fast and good care afterward. She might not even lose her looks.

"If we're collecting prisoners, how about patching up our friend there?" the Shadow asked. "I'll search below."

Bolan had applied dressings when the Shadow came up from below. "Nothing left down below but guns, ammo, some food and the stuff they were using on Gloria." There was no mistaking the tightly controlled rage in the man's voice.

"Okay. Let's bring in the Huey. I'll work on Gloria."

"Gutsy broad, that Gloria," the Shadow said. He sounded almost tender. "Guess they figured out what she did, getting the kids away."

"Kids..." came a small voice, almost a child's itself. "Kids—got to get them away. The mountain farm...nobody comes back...nobody from the mountain. Oh, God, it hurts."

"Gloria," the Shadow said urgently, "the mountain house. Who's going there? Who?"

"Donna. Donna—the Capezzis— Don Marco's there." The words ended in a gasp of pain.

"The mountain farm," the Shadow said slowly. "Stormgren Farm. That makes sense."

"The Capezzi safehouse out near the Olympics?" Bolan asked.

"Got it." The Shadow straightened up, then laughed harshly. "We know they've got Donna there, and they don't know we know."

He bent quickly and heaved the unconscious gunman down the hatch. Bolan stared at his partner as the hardman crashed to the planks.

"We know where Donna is. That means we don't need any prisoners. Not these—things."

The rage in the Shadow's voice was almost palpable. Before Bolan could lift a finger, the man had put two slugs into the wounded mafioso.

The Executioner decided that he wasn't going to risk getting Gloria killed by confronting this cold-blooded murderer. He'd have time for that later.

"Ready?" the Shadow asked from the pilothouse door. "Thanh's called the Huey. He'll be up in about ten minutes."

Bolan nodded curtly. He saw that the Shadow was holding the Hi-Power in one hand and one of the demolition charges in the other. As the warrior lifted the unconscious Gloria, the Shadow tossed the bomb down the hatchway.

He must have set the fuse very short; they'd just climbed aboard the cruiser when the explosive went off. Most of the pilothouse turned back into the lumber the houseboat used to carry. Thick black smoke rolled up from a dozen places as ruptured tanks spilled diesel oil onto open flames.

Then Thanh swung the wheel hard over and opened the throttles. The diesels roared, and in five minutes the houseboat, already lower in the water, was lost in the darkness and the patches of fog.

"SO THAT'S IT," Bolan concluded. "I can't give you a breakdown on the percentages of Capezzi and Mangnani soldiers. I know we didn't recognize any of the top men from either Family."

Hal Brognola was silent for a moment, then said, "Striker, you sound weary."

"It's been a long night. The only one of us who's going to catch up on sleep is Gloria."

"How is she?"

"The doctor says there may not even be any major scarring. The people who worked her over were pretty much amateurs. Also, we asked her a few questions. She said that Goss—or the one who looks like Goss—joined in. But he didn't look like he was enjoying it. She also thinks he might have been the one who gave her the double dose of morphine. That might have saved her life by making the goon squad think she was dying."

"I wonder what side our friendly Marine corporal thinks he's on?" Brognola mused. "Never mind, I hope we'll soon be able to ask him."

"With any luck, we should."

"You're moving out tomorrow?"

"You mean today. Yes. Right now both Families are off balance. Don Marco's going to be too mad to see straight. Don Ettore might be scared. The Zorinos are going to sit this one out, at least until they see who's winning.

"There's also Gloria to think about. If we give Don Marco a single extra day, she could be in danger. As long as Don Marco's alive, the Federal Witness Protection Program won't be enough. Locking her in a safe at Fort Knox might help, but I wouldn't even bet on that."

"I wouldn't argue with your tactics, Striker. But it isn't the tactical situation that's bugging you, is it?"

"I suppose not. There's the question about the Shadow and Tom Westin."

"If Don Pietro insists on letting Westin go along..."

"He does."

"Then try to keep him out of the line of fire. Getting him wasted could get this whole thing into the newspapers. This will make some very important people unhappy. We want to keep them happy."

"Understood. And the Shadow?"

"Think he's about to turn?"

"Not until Donna Westin's safe, and maybe nothing that simple even then. I just wonder if something's working at him that may wreck his judgment at the wrong time."

"Judgment or no, you asked for him, so Don Pietro's going to insist that he hang in there." Brognola was silent for long enough to make Bolan wonder if he'd hung up. Then, "Striker, I'm not putting the Shadow up for a knighthood...."

"Go on."

"What happened to Gloria might have just pushed a button in the Shadow. This is mostly rumor, and we didn't even get most of the rumor until after we ran up the file on him, but it seems that about six years ago, he was sweet on a girl working for the Capezzis. He wanted her out, she wanted out, Don Marco didn't want her out. So he sent Frank Garrado over. She died in the Emergency Room, and I understand two nurses fainted when they saw her."

"Six years ago?" Bolan said. "Frank Garrado was killed—"

"Exactly. My hunch is that Frank Garrado was a private hit by the Shadow. Don Pietro may have squared Capezzi, or he might have just told Don Marco to pee up a rope. The Britos had a lot more muscle then."

"So the Shadow likes clean kills? You're right, I won't put him up for a knighthood. The people left behind miss the dead just as much. I don't have the feeling he ever thought of that."

"Neither do I," Brognola said. "Any more to get off your chest, or shall we call it a night?"

"Let's pack it in."

16

The Boot looked in the rearview mirror of Don Marco's Cadillac and frowned. Then he tapped the driver on the shoulder.

"Slow down. That rag-gnawed Lincoln of Don Ettore's is going to have to back and fill to make the turn."

In the back seat the Capezzi capo cursed under his breath. Certainly meeting at Stormgren Farm had seemed a good idea when he proposed it. The place was well out of town, easy to defend with enough men and private enough for anything they might wish to do with Donna Westin.

Unfortunately Don Marco hadn't reckoned that Don Ettore loved his comforts. Specifically the comfort of his custom-furnished Lincoln limousine. He'd refused the offer of one of Don Marco's Cadillacs for himself, even one for his men. The Mangnanis would come to the meeting in their Lincolns, which could barely handle the winding mountain road.

Don Marco hoped that Don Ettore's black-and-red monster had good brakes for the return trip. Or did he hope that?

It wouldn't hurt the Capezzis if Don Ettore died in a way that couldn't be blamed on them. It would mean fewer hands thrust out for the money when Don Pietro paid it. It would mean no one to tell the Commission in New York about the Capezzis' war on the Brito relatives, if it came to that.

But it would also mean fewer guns to fight off the menacing figure the Britos had conjured up as if by magic. No, only by money. It would be as well if Don Ettore and good soldiers like Lucco Contamine survived until the Executioner or his ghost were no longer a danger.

A shadow passed across the road, and Don Marco started.

"Just a helicopter," the Boot said. "They're like dragonflies around here. The lumber companies, the crop dusters, the Forestry Service—everybody and their aunt has one."

"Just as long as none of the aunts come calling without an invitation, they can fly around all day and all night," Don Marco said. He knew he was blustering to cover his uneasiness. He also knew that the Boot was aware of his capo's feelings.

The Boot was technically almost as accomplished a hitter as Pescaglia. But in showing respect to his capo, he would never be Antonio's equal. That was another matter on which Don Marco would have satisfaction.

IF ANYTHING, the Huey was even noisier than it had been the night before. Bolan had to shout in Tom Westin's ear to be sure he was being heard.

At least nobody else was going to overhear the conversation. Al Torstensson and the Shadow were at the front of the cabin, checking their weapons and gear. Monty Pelham was at the controls, looking grim. The flying conditions were good, but he knew he'd be support and backup again and didn't like it.

"Dammit, either let me go in on the ground or let me steal a Huey Cobra and help that way!" he'd said to Bolan and Torstensson.

"Three reasons, Monty," the security chief said. "One is we need airlift. Two is a Huey Cobra would be overkill. Three is I say so."

"Yeah, sure," Pelham grumbled, trying to grin.

"Don't forget, Gloria might owe you her life," Bolan said. "She certainly owes you her chances of a quick recovery. You're carrying your weight and then some, Monty."

Pelham still wasn't happy, but he'd play his assigned role. Bolan wished he could be as sure about Tom Westin. The role he'd wanted to assign the writer was staying at least fifty miles from the rescue, but Don Pietro had shot that one down.

Now Bolan was trying to be sure Westin would do his job as backup and security, an assignment he shared with Al Torstensson. It would strain Boeing's patience to have Al on the mission at all, but if he was identified at the site of the shooting, it would mean at least his job.

"Don't sweat it, Mr. Belasko," Westin said. He adjusted his glasses and bent over his rifle. It was a Match grade M-14, with a four-power sight, a glass-bedded action and picked rounds in four 20-round magazines. Seeing that weapon, Bolan suspected that Westin's popular thrillers had given him more clout in military circles than he'd let on.

"I'm not sweating anything," Bolan replied. He hoped he sounded truthful. "You're the one who ought to be sweating. Getting involved with a fight against the Families—"

"Is risky, I know. Look, I researched the Mafia pretty thoroughly for *Dead Man's Gambit*. Not just the Families here in the States, but the Sicilian connection. I know how they handle funds. I also know what they think of a man who won't protect his wife, but lets others do the work for him. Donna will be in more danger if I wimp out than if I come along. Besides, if everything goes as planned, there won't be enough Capezzis left to worry anybody. Not me, not Gloria, not those Vietnamese you're so careful not to mention."

Bolan hadn't read any of Westin's novels. When a man's daily life was a thriller, he didn't need to read them. But he'd seen Westin sighting in the M-14 and a Combat Magnum on the range. Ten out of ten in the kill zone at three hundred yards with the rifle—nine out of ten at seventy-five yards with the Magnum. He was also built like Conan the Barbarian.

"And if it doesn't?"

"I have to live with myself, even if I also have to live without Donna. Remember what I told Don Pietro about the kids' questions?"

"I remember. But I also remember what a rifle instructor once told me. 'Don't ever confuse skill on the range with the ability to kill a man, until you've done it.' What if you have a live target in your sights?''

Westin snapped the magazine in place, then started polishing the lenses of the sight with a soft cloth. "Mr. Belasko, I'll have to pass on that one. All I can say is, anybody who shows up in my sights on this mission is likely to be somebody who wanted to kill my wife. That might do something about my freezing on the trigger."

At least Westin wasn't promising more than he thought he could perform. As a writer he might be a little better at analyzing his own reactions than most people. Bolan decided to drop it once he'd asked Al Torstensson to keep a close eye on Westin.

DONNA WESTIN RAN a finger around the inside of her jeans, where they chafed. She did it carefully, turning away from the hardman by the basement door.

The jeans were hopelessly too tight, and the sweater was just as hopelessly too large. But they'd made it clear it was that or nothing, and she'd had enough of wearing nothing in front of her kidnappers. It didn't bother Gloria, at least until they started in on her, but then Gloria had been a hooker for ten years. In that life a woman got used to wearing her bare skin or she got out.

A knock on the door, and the hardman rose, drawing a pistol. Donna wished she'd gone over more of her husband's gun books. Not that recognizing the Mafia's weapons would help her much, but it might be useful research material for Tom when she got clear.

A shudder ran through the woman, and she sat down faster than she'd intended. Who was she kidding? She had less than an even chance of getting out of here at all.

She could see that in Don Marco's face every time he looked at her. She could see that both he and the Boot would enjoy working her over or worse. Don Marco wanted her father's money. He also wanted vengeance on his old rival, for beating him so often and then walking away. Don Pietro couldn't walk away from his daughter's being scarred for life.

The door opened, letting in that ex-Marine, Goss. He was carrying a covered tray and handed it to the hardman. Donna felt like sticking out her tongue at Goss. He'd seemed to be on her side, or at least not completely on Don Marco's, at first. Then she saw him join in on Gloria. After that, she knew he was as dirty as the rest of them.

She turned her back on the hardman as he thanked Goss and started on his lunch.

THE FIVE MEN KNELT around an aerial photograph of Stormgren Farm. The eyes of four followed Bolan's finger.

"The Shadow and I take the farm. One of us pins everybody down by taking a high position, probably the water tank."

The Shadow frowned. "The shape it's in, I don't think it could hold up a large dog."

"We'll see," Bolan said. "Use your judgment." He hoped the Shadow's judgment would be in favor of staying a good guy until this mission was over. He couldn't do much more than hope, a situation he disliked.

But likes or dislikes didn't count here. The only thing that counted was getting Donna Westin safely away from the farm and its garrison of killers.

"The other moves into the house, springs Donna and gets her to safety. Then he returns, covers the withdrawal of the cover man, and we all join up with the blocking party."

He turned to Torstensson and Westin. "That's you. You can't afford to be recognized at the farm, so you hold the road. Probably here." He tapped the map where the contour lines showed a steep ridge overlooking a hairpin bend in the road. "Anybody coming through here will have to slow down or wind up in the ravine."

"What about the road uphill?" Torstensson asked. He traced the line that showed an unimproved road winding up through the firs to the crest of Stormgren Hill.

"They can't take the limos up that grade," Bolan replied. "If they come up with the four-wheeler, that's Monty's job. Block them, then either call in help to clean them out or jump in the Huey and lift out. That'll have to be a judgment call."

Pelham's judgment at least could be trusted. So could his firepower. He had the hangar assassin's M-16, as well as his own Bulldog, and enough ammunition to keep a squad going in a firefight.

"Why just two people into the farm?" Westin asked. He took off his glasses and polished them again, even though he'd done it three times on the flight in.

The man was nervous but trying to be polite, Bolan decided.

"If we have surprise, two men will be enough. If we don't, two hundred won't be. Taking more than two men increases the risk of our being spotted on the way in."

Westin put his glasses back on and looked at the ground. He obviously wasn't happy, but Bolan wasn't asking him to be.

"How are we going to be sure Donna isn't in a car coming down the road?" Westin asked.

The Shadow threw first Westin, then Bolan, a sharp look. Bolan's eyes met those of his two professional allies, Torstensson and Pelham.

"The first thing the cover man's going to do is take out their wheels," the Shadow said. "So there shouldn't be any cars coming downhill in the first place."

"But if you don't get lucky—"

"We don't rely on luck the way writers do," the Shadow said.

Westin had the sense not to touch a gun, but if looks could kill he wouldn't have needed one. The Shadow's hand was halfway to his Browning before the Executioner's glare halted the motion.

"If you gentlemen will open your ears and close your mouths, I believe Mike was coming to that," Torstensson said. He didn't look at either man.

"Right," Bolan said. "We'll have a visual and a radio signal. Visual signal is a red smoke flare. Radio code is 'geranium.' Either one means that a car coming downhill might have Donna in it, so let it pass."

"Let it pass?" Westin repeated, his voice rising.

"All those books—" the Shadow started to reply.

"Knock it off," Bolan said, and got at least a sullen silence. For a moment he wished he was about the size and strength of King Kong. He might be able to rescue Donna Westin by the simple method of tearing the farmhouse apart. He could certainly pick up Westin and the Shadow and crack their heads together.

"There are a lot of things we can do to get your wife back even if they get her away from the farm," Pelham said. "There's not a goddamned thing we can do if she's burning at the bottom of that ravine!"

The point seemed to get through. Westin subsided. The Shadow pulled his G-3 out of the bag and began checking the bolt.

Bolan and Torstensson exchanged hand signals. They had their own codes, worked out for just this kind of situation and unknown to both Westin and the Shadow. Bolan couldn't refuse to let the Shadow have a radio or a red flare. That would be starting a war with the Shadow before they'd finished the one against the Capezzis. He could certainly keep the Shadow from sending a false signal that would sign Donna Westin's death warrant.

Why the Shadow might want to do this, Bolan didn't know and didn't have time to guess. In any case, it didn't matter, as long as the Shadow didn't do it.

Ten minutes of checking weapons and equipment was enough to cool tempers all around. The Shadow and Westin even shook hands briefly as they stood up.

Monty Pelham vanished into the trees uphill, heading for the Huey, while Torstensson led Westin toward their ambush position on the road.

"Let's do a real good job on those cars," the Shadow said as he slung his rifle. "I'd kind of like to be able to call the other two up to cover our asses."

"You and me both," Bolan replied. "Monty can pull us out faster if he has to make only one pickup. But if we can't, we can't."

And if they were in three groups rather than one, the Shadow couldn't so easily wipe out the rest of the party. Any double cross would warn Bolan first—and the Executioner was the most experienced, the most alert and the hardest to kill.

The two big men moved twenty yards apart and headed into the forest.

17

Bolan and the Shadow covered the two miles to the farm in less than half an hour. They spent another ten minutes studying it.

Nobody at the farm spotted the two men during the ten minutes. Both wore camouflage fatigues and had their faces lightly smeared with combat cosmetics. They'd taped down or left behind all their metal gear and darkened the surfaces of their weapons as much as they could. It wasn't as thorough a job as Bolan would have liked, but both men could have stepped into the middle of a field exercise with nobody raising an eyebrow.

They saw no sign of Donna Westin. The Capezzis had no reason to keep her anywhere in the open.

In fact, they now had one extra reason to keep her hidden. Two Lincolns that Bolan recognized were parked in front of the farmhouse. Both of them were Mangnani wheels, and the limousine with the red leather roof was Don Ettore Mangnani's personal transportation.

"Not good," the Shadow whispered.

"Not as bad as you think," Bolan replied. The Shadow frowned. Bolan continued, "The two Families haven't been friends in the past. I doubt if they're friends now. That means their soldiers won't be trained to work together."

"That can't happen overnight, true. But has it been overnight?"

"You'd know that better than I."

"Maybe."

Bolan decided that was all the answer he was going to get. It might even be all he needed. If the Britos had learned anything about a Mangnani-Capezzi alliance and held out on him, it would endanger Donna Westin. It wasn't likely that Don Pietro would change his mind on that point at the last moment. Bolan wished he could be as sure about the Shadow.

The council of war took two minutes, and the two men held it mostly in facial expressions, shrugs and gestures. The wind was blowing away from the farm, and the sentries would be city men who didn't know the noises of the countryside, but why take chances?

In two more minutes they began their final stalk. Bolan cut sharply to the left to approach one sentry post under cover of a ravine overgrown with saplings. When he'd taken out the sentry, the Shadow would slip through the gap and find his high ground inside the farm.

Bolan slid down into the ravine and slipped through the tangled branches and springy trunks. Wet leaves slapped him in the face and soaked his black-stocking cap.

In five minutes he was on the far side of the ravine, less than fifty feet from the sentry. From a hundred yards to his right he saw a hand flicker. The Shadow was ready.

Bolan started to crawl up to the lip of the ravine. Forty feet, thirty, twenty—he paused to draw the silenced Beretta—the sentry was actually turning his back on the Executioner....

"Hi, Fredo," the man called.

"Keep your eyes on— Hey, intrud—"

Fredo died with his warning half-finished, as Bolan took him out of the play. The other sentry whirled like a dervish, trying to look in all directions at once and missing Bolan completely. Fredo's warning came too late; the man died with three 9 mm tumblers drilled into his chest.

But the other gunners had heard the warning and reacted to it. Bolan saw two men rush around the farmhouse, well out of range of the Beretta. He was shifting to the Desert Eagle when the men got a reminder about the range of G-3 assault rifles.

The Shadow's burst chopped both men down as they ran. Then Bolan saw him sprinting toward the farm, vaulting the rotten fence without breaking stride and vanishing around the old chicken coops. In that direction the highest point was the roof of the barn rather than the water tower. Somebody on the tower could still shoot down at the Shadow, if he could get up on the tower in the first place....

Bolan decided that it was his job to see that nobody could.

Dodging from tree to tree, crouching whenever he was in the open, Bolan closed on the farm. The big .44

filled his right hand, and he'd opened the flap of the pouch of grenades.

Losing surprise didn't mean losing the battle, if victory was getting Donna Westin away safely. Just possibly the Mangnanis might be willing to turn her over, if he promised to let them get away. Their presence here might be turned into an asset.

Bolan hated the thought of a Mafia Don and his soldiers getting away once they were in his sights, but he hated the thought of Donna Westin dying at Don Marco's hands much more.

DONNA WESTIN'S KNEES GAVE under her as she heard the firing outside. As she heard men running and shouting, she gripped the back of a sagging rattan chair and lowered herself into it.

The guns had come out. In five more minutes she'd be out of this basement, alive or dead.

She'd made up her mind yesterday that she wouldn't let them do to her what they'd done to Gloria. Don Marco had boasted at length of what he would do, of how other women had looked, of how criminal her father was being to let her face this danger out of greed.

"Criminal." That was a fine word for Don Marco to use. When she saw Tom again she'd have to tell him about this perfect example of the pot calling the kettle black.

A sob rose in her throat and threatened to choke her as she thought of not seeing Tom again.

The cellar door flew open so violently that the lock clanged as it struck the wall, and two men stormed down the stairs. Donna cringed as she recognized the Boot in the lead. Then she saw Goss, the Marine, behind the Boot.

The Boot was too flattered by the cringing to notice her look at Goss. He aimed a Hi-Power at her with one hand and held out handcuffs with the other. They were the same viciously tight ones she'd had on before.

"Turn around, real slow, and you walk out of here. Any fancy stuff, and Don Marco says I can start hurting you."

Which was the best possible reason for the "fancy stuff," except that she wasn't absolutely sure she could force the Boot to kill her, and there was Goss to consider.

She considered Goss. The Boot didn't and paid the price. Goss drew his .45 and shot the Boot through the head. The huge slug went in the man's right temple and exited his left, most of the skull going with it.

Donna was close enough to be spattered with blood, brains and chunks of bone. She lost her grip on the chair, fell to her knees and threw up what felt like everything she'd eaten since she was kidnapped.

Goss let her finish vomiting, then pulled her briskly to her feet. When he was sure she could stand alone, he handed her the Boot's Hi-Power.

"Can you use this?"

"Yes."

He pointed back toward the far rear right-hand corner of the cellar. "If you go back that way, there's a little space where the foundation's shifted. Squeeze into that, and it's pretty good odds they won't be able to find you."

"And if they do?"

"Then they can't come at you too easy. You've got a gun, and the mag's full. I loaded it for the son of a bitch myself." To Donna Westin, it sounded as if having to wait on the Boot was the worst insult that Goss had suffered.

She followed the Marine's gesture. The crack was there, and the space beyond it. But try as she could, she was just about a quarter-inch too big to get through.

But a quarter-inch was just about the thickness of her clothes. She jerked the sweater over her head, then sat down to struggle out of the jeans.

She ignored Goss's round eyes. He'd made his bones, all right, but not for the Families—he'd be as dead as she could be when Don Marco caught up with him. She finished stripping, stuffed the clothes through the crack and tried to follow them.

She was missing a good deal of skin from various parts of her anatomy when she'd finished squeezing in, but she was inside the space. She could neither sit, stand, nor lie, and she hoped leg cramps wouldn't drive her to betraying herself. But she was out of sight of anyone who wasn't standing directly in front of the crack and looking into it.

Right now that was Goss. She was just about to tell him that the peep show was over when someone shouted from upstairs.

Goss replied in horrible Italian that the Marine tried to shoot Donna and was shot in turn.

Donna cringed at the accent, went cold at the silence from the top of the stairs, then cringed again as

the door opened. Goss's .45 bucked in his hand four
times, drowning out the shouts of the men at the top
of the stairs. She couldn't see how many he hit, but she
heard three screams and saw one outflung hand.

She also saw bullets from at least two guns rip into
Goss, so that for a moment he seemed to spout blood
from a dozen places. Then, as if the blood had been
keeping him upright, he collapsed. A little more blood
trickled out of his mouth as he tried to raise the .45
again. Then his hand dropped back, and the .45 clattered out of limp fingers.

In her hiding place Donna heard footsteps on the
stairs. She chambered a round in the Hi-Power,
snapped off the safety and held it ready in one hand.

The footsteps came on. Now they were halfway
down the stairs.

Donna stuffed the other hand into her mouth to
keep from screaming. She reminded herself that a full
magazine in a Hi-Power meant thirteen 9 mm rounds,
enough for a big dent in the Capezzis and a final bullet for herself if it came to that. She decided that she'd
never again think the "Save the last bullet for yourself" business in Western novels was silly.

The footsteps reached the bottom of the stairs. At
least two men, she decided. She heard low voices, one
of them cursing.

Then more shots erupted upstairs. She heard a
scream, a long burst of automatic fire and the whoosh
of a gas tank igniting.

Both men were now cursing. They were also running up the stairs as fast as they could. Donna listened to them go, then slumped against the rough

stone. She'd never before had so much gooseflesh *and* so much sweat on her at the same time.

IT SEEMED TO BOLAN that the farm was three miles wide, and it took him half an hour to cross it. He knew this was the distortion of time and space that hits anyone caught up in a firefight, and ignored it.

What he couldn't ignore was the sheer number of hardmen traversing the farm. Sometimes it seemed there were enough for more than two Families. Having Mangnani soldiers on hand would add to the enemy's confusion, but it might also add too much to their firepower.

Bolan moved with the Beretta in one hand and the Desert Eagle in the other. The 93-R had now traded its silencer for its shoulder stock. The selector was set to 3-round bursts.

The Executioner was ready to engage targets of opportunity, but he wasn't seeking a shoot-out now. The less he fired, the harder it would be for the enemy to keep track of him. It wouldn't matter if the attack was no longer a surprise so long as he reached the farmhouse before Don Marco could organize a reception committee.

From the top of the barn, the Shadow's G-3 was doing a fine job of keeping Mafia heads down and occasionally blowing them off. Assault rifles weren't basically precision weapons, but in the hands of a master marksman they would do everything needed here.

So far the Shadow seemed to be aiming mostly at people. He'd either changed his mind about taking out the wheels, or the firepower from below was keeping him too busy to shoot at anything that couldn't shoot back.

Bolan got as far as the last of the row of chicken coops before being spotted. The coop was so thoroughly rotted that its walls were more open air than boards. He crawled inside the coop, into a floor still reeking with the droppings of chickens long gone. Bullets chopped through boards over his head and added a few more holes to the roof, but missed him. Rolling onto his left side, he saw a shadow pass by the end of the coop.

The shadow wore a windbreaker and jeans and had an AR-15 slung across its back. As he reached the base of the water tower, he stretched upward and began to climb.

Tactics weren't completely a closed book to the hardmen. Some of them were going to pin Bolan down, while a friend climbed the water tower and sniped the Shadow. Then the Families would hold the high ground against only one opponent, and Donna Westin would be in serious trouble.

The hardmen had forgotten one elementary tactical principle, though—always allow for the worst your opponent can do. In this case, Bolan couldn't get a better firing position without exposing himself. But he could throw a grenade.

Actually he threw two—one a yellow smoke grenade, the other a frag—at the man climbing the water tower.

The man flew off the tower in bloody shreds, screaming all the way down, followed by chunks of timber. Then the whole tower shuddered, tilted and collapsed in a roar of cracking wood and a cloud of dust. Stagnant rainwater poured over Bolan.

He shifted position again, scrambling into the wreckage of the tower. From behind a tilted support he had a good angle with the Desert Eagle on the nearest man trying to pin him down. The first Magnum round blew the man into the open, kicking and thrashing. The second stopped him dead.

Then red fireflies danced in the farmyard as the Shadow opened up with a magazine that was one-third tracer. The fireflies danced toward the rear of one of the Capezzi Cadillacs and found the gas tank.

A ball of orange flame erupted, half hiding, half lifting the Cadillac. A hardman stepped out the farmhouse door and gaped; Bolan sighted in and shot him at near-maximum range.

They were winning, the Shadow and the Executioner. But the battle wasn't over, and Donna Westin could still lose.

To Don Ettore Mangnani, it seemed that his alliance with Don Marco Capezzi would soon be worthless. Nothing was of value to a dead man, which he'd be if he didn't leave this house as soon as possible.

But Don Marco could do nothing but rave about how they must find Donna Westin. He was looking about wildly, as if he had Superman's X-ray vision and could see through the walls to where she hid.

He was also waving around a stainless-steel .45 which didn't bother Don Ettore as much as it might have. Don Ettore was very proud of his reputation for no longer bothering to carry weapons. That reputation might be useful today.

"Bring your men in here now, Don Ettore!" the Capezzi capo screamed. "Mine will cover yours. Then we'll have the strength to tear the house apart and find that bitch!"

It took a moment for Don Ettore to realize that Capezzi meant Donna Westin. He looked at Lucco Contamine, who seemed to share his distaste for staying and dying with the Capezzis.

Good. His first soldier was better than anyone the Capezzis had left, far better than Don Marco.

"My men are in position already to cover the retreat of yours," Don Ettore snapped. "We have more long-range weapons. So why—"

"Then use them to shoot that bastard off the barn roof!" Don Marco screamed, even more hysterical than before. "Once he's done, we can move freely. Or pin him down while we find Donna. If we pull her out and start on her, they'll surely hold their fire."

Don Ettore wasn't so sure of that. He was quite sure that beginning the rough stuff on Donna Westin would destroy their negotiating position. The *rest* of their negotiating position, he corrected himself. They didn't have much left, and if this attack continued to eat their soldiers they'd have none.

Not to mention no lives, which Don Ettore discovered wasn't as small a matter as he'd thought. No one in his Family was the stuff of which capos were made. Especially they wouldn't be the capos to put a battered Family back together, heal its wounds, replace its

dead soldiers and win for it domination in the Northwest.

Don Ettore not only wanted to live; he *had* to.

"Lucco, order the riflemen to pin down the man on
the barn. The rest, into the limousines. Leave room for
any of Don—"

"You coward!" Don Marco was barely coherent.

"We're not going to leave you behind, if that's what
you're afraid of," Contamine snapped. "You and any
of your men who want to join us—"

Don Marco was too furious to speak. He wasn't too
furious to draw down on Don Ettore.

This was a mistake, for two reasons. One was that
Don Ettore, contrary to his custom, was armed. The
mini .22 he carried in an inside breast pocket had very
little range, but he was standing practically nose-to-
nose with his target. At that range the little revolver
was quite effective.

Don Ettore might still have died with his former ally
without Don Marco's second mistake. He drew when
he was blocking the fire of his only soldier in the
room. The man saw that he didn't have a clear shot at
Don Ettore and took a vital fraction of a second
switching to Contamine.

That was enough for Contamine to make the fast-
est draw of his life and punch three .41 Magnum soft-
noses into the hardman's chest and throat. He hit the
floor a moment later than his capo, but he was dead
long before Don Marco stopped thrashing about.

Two more Capezzi soldiers stopped tearing the cellar apart and dashed up the stairs—straight into fire
from Don Ettore, using Don Marco's .45, Lucco

Contamine and another Mangnani soldier. One of the Capezzis sprawled on the floor; the other fell back down the stairs and lay at the foot, screaming until blood-filled lungs choked him into silence.

By now the Mangnani riflemen were blazing away in fine fashion. Don Ettore listened and heard no answering fire. He doubted that the Executioner and the other men were dead, but perhaps they might be cautious for a few minutes.

An idea bubbled up in Don Ettore's mind, and he smiled.

"Lucco. Whichever cars we take, open the trunks."

"The trunks?" Contamine obviously thought that his capo had gone mad, just like Don Marco.

"Yes. Those men may pursue us if they think we have Donna Westin in one of the trunks. If they think she's still here, in danger from the Capezzis—"

"Ah." Contamine nodded.

"When we reach the main road, we can close them. We do not, after all, wish to be pulled up by the state police."

"The state police..." Contamine's heavy shoulders were shaking with silent laughter as he headed for the door. Don Ettore sat down, because parts of his body were shaking, too, starting with his legs.

"Are you well, Don Ettore?" the soldier remaining on guard asked.

"Well enough."

The truth indeed. He was alive, which was more than he had expected five minutes ago. He might even get off Stormgren Hill and back to Seattle alive.

Then he'd have a good many possibilities, including rescuing Donna Westin from the Capezzis, if they still had her. That should be worth some of Don Pietro's money, if not the whole ten million.

Better yet, he wouldn't have to divide it with the Capezzis now. And he would give the Zorinos, that miserable excuse for a Family, a single penny only if they agreed to his leadership all over Puget Sound. For Don Ettore Mangnani, "snatching victory from the jaws of defeat" was no longer merely a phrase.

18

Bolan could only hope that the Shadow was still alive. The rifles aimed at him included at least one M-16, and the mafiosi seemed to have a truckload of ammunition. He hadn't seen or heard from his partner for at least five minutes, an eternity in a firefight.

At least the hardmen were still shooting mostly at the barn. That meant they thought the Shadow was still alive. It also meant that most of their attention and firepower was directed away from the Executioner.

He wasn't in a good firing position now, in the ruins of the water tower. The cars and bushes hid the soldiers too well, from too many angles. But with their attention elsewhere, he could move more safely.

Not safely enough, as he discovered a moment later. A wild burst from the M-16 came as close as if the man had been aiming. Bolan felt the wind of bullets on his cheek and throat and promptly hit the dirt again.

Time to unlimber the Weatherby. Bolan unslung the big rifle and felt in his pocket for the hand-loaded incendiary rounds. There was nothing like seeing a retreat cut off to bring men to reason—or at least out into the open where they could be killed.

Shoot or negotiate. Bolan would do whichever one was the best for Donna Westin, as long as she was alive.

If she wasn't, none of the mafiosi would leave Stormgren Hill alive if Bolan could arrange it. If he couldn't, they'd walk the streets under a death sentence handed down by no judge and subject to no appeal.

The rifle fire was slackening now. Bolan started to move again. Then he froze as the two Lincolns started to back away from the house. From bushes by the road, the M-16 opened up again, sending bullets thunking into the timbers around Bolan.

As if the same finger had pressed both buttons, the Lincolns' trunks flew open together. Bolan had a good look at luxuriously upholstered compartments that held practically nothing. No weapons, no tools, hardly any baggage except a couple of briefcases. Nothing large enough to hold a body, and no Donna Westin, alive or dead, intact or in pieces.

One of the Lincolns slowed briefly to let the M-16 gunner leap inside. Then both were rolling off down the hill, screened by the trees from both the Shadow and the Executioner.

As the tail of the second Lincoln disappeared around the bend, Bolan's partner came back to life. Red smoke blossomed on the roof of the barn, rose straight until it reached the wind above the trees, then spread out. A great red scar stretched across the sky, signaling to the ambush team below that Donna Westin was in one of the cars.

Bolan's legs were already driving him toward the house. Now his mind raced as fast as his legs. Had the Shadow seen something his partner hadn't, such as Donna Westin being bundled into one of the Lincolns in men's clothing? Not impossible.

It also wasn't impossible that the man had started to change sides, giving a false signal to let the men in the Lincolns get away.

Nothing was impossible, in fact, except knowing where Donna Westin was before he found her. Bolan took a short detour to make sure she wasn't where he'd seen the M-16 rifleman, then closed on the house.

It looked empty and lifeless, with the particularly dismal kind of lifelessness that comes when evil men die in what was once a home. Bolan still approached it as cautiously as if all Don Marco's soldiers together waited there armed with machine guns.

He also threw an occasional look backward to check on his partner. The red smoke was fading now; if they hadn't seen the signal downhill, they weren't going to.

If there were still live enemies holed up in some of the other farm buildings, it made sense for the Shadow to go on holding the high ground. It also made sense for him to stay up high if he wanted a good shot at the Executioner as soon as he learned Donna Westin's fate.

Bolan felt the flesh between his shoulder blades tense at the last thought. No amount of experience, no amount of skill and no amount of self-control could make a man comfortable with treachery.

DOWNHILL, TOM WESTIN FELT Al Torstensson grab his arm.

"Come on, Tom. We're going to shift over to the other side of the ridge."

"What the hell for? You saw the signal."

"Yeah, I saw the signal," the security chief said slowly. "I also saw that from over where we're going, we can get a second shot at the cars."

"Why? Donna's in there, we agreed on the signal. It won't matter how many shots we get, there's no safe way—"

"No safe way, if that signal was right."

"I don't follow you."

"You'd better, 'cause you're a better rifle shot than I am."

Westin grabbed Torstensson's arm. The security man shook off the writer's grip as if he'd been a mosquito. Westin glared.

"You explain, or I'm not going."

"I shouldn't have to explain this to a thriller writer, but I will. Ever heard of private codes?"

"Private— You and Mike Belasko?"

"Right. We go back a way. Enough so that I want to double-check with him about who's in those cars."

It made sense. A hell of a lot of sense, when you considered that the Shadow was probably Mafia. Everybody seemed to skate around that point when Westin was around, but his research had been useful there, too.

Westin rose without slinging his rifle.

"You might need both hands to get over the crest," Torstensson said.

"Maybe. But the SAS always carries their weapons in both hands when they're in Indian country. It just occurred to me that some of our Mafia friends might have staked out the ambush points above the road. If we run into any of them—"

Torstensson frowned at being told his business by an amateur. Then the frown left his face, and he drew his Blackhawk as they started to climb the ridge.

THE FIRST THING BOLAN MET when he entered the farmhouse was a litter of bodies. He'd just identified Don Marco's when he met the second thing.

It was a burst of fire from an Uzi.

The warrior had the gunner located as he dropped, rolled and came up with the Desert Eagle in both hands. The .44 Magnum sent echoes bouncing around the living room and slugs tearing up the stairs. A hardman toppled through the railing in a cloud of dust and splinters and hit the floor, most of his chest gone.

Bolan collected all the loose guns he could find and started up the stairs. He searched the sparsely furnished upper floor without finding either Donna Westin or any more opponents, then climbed up to the attic. He drew a blank there, too, and decided it was time to check in with the Shadow and find out if his partner had seen anything.

All he got was static.

On the way down Bolan was careful not to pass in front of any window with a view of the barn. This slowed him down a bit, but he was still in the basement five minutes after entering the house.

Bolan was kneeling beside the body of Corporal Goss when he heard a faint scratching noise. It sounded like rats, but then it came again, louder, and the Executioner thought he heard a moan.

"Donna Westin?" he called.

The sudden silence told him almost as much as a reply.

"Where are you?"

More silence.

"It's safe. I'm a friend, and both Families are dead, pinned down or running for their lives."

He thought he heard a sigh, then realized that something had slipped all their minds. After days of brutal captivity ending in a firefight, Donna Westin was probably in no mood to trust anyone.

How could he prove he was a friend? Bolan's mind raced back over the past few days, calling up his conversations with Tom Westin.

"Tom says if you get back safe, you'll never have to clean up Ricky's Lego blocks again."

"Oh, God!" It was partly a prayer, partly a scream and partly a sob. The next moment Donna Westin was wriggling out of a crack in the walls, wearing nothing but dirt, and sweat. She held a Browning Hi-Power in one hand.

Bolan noted that the hand was steady and the safety off. He also realized that he'd been standing right in front of the crack in the wall. If Donna Westin had decided he was another mafioso, the Executioner's career would have been over.

"No wonder nobody found you," he said. "Better hold on to that gun while I call some friends."

"Friends?" She sounded as if she'd never heard of such a thing. Then he could see her force her nerves to stop jumping and her voice to something like normal. "Call anybody you please. I'm going to get some clothes on."

Bolan bounded up the stairs two at a time. If he could just find a clear spot to transmit where the Shadow couldn't see him...

AL TORSTENSSON HELD UP a hand, then held the radio to his ear.

"That's it," he said. "The red smoke was wrong."

"The Shadow?" Westin asked.

"Likely enough," the security man replied. "But I got Mike's code message. There's nobody but bad guys in those limos coming down. Now, if they just take their time speeding up after they get around the bend..."

Westin was the first to spot the two Lincolns rounding the hairpin curve. They seemed to be crawling. He sighted in on the second one, figuring that it was more likely to hold one of the Dons.

The cross hairs centered on the driver. Westin swallowed, started to squeeze the trigger, then felt his muscles refusing to obey his brain.

Then muscles and brain both screamed "Stop!" as a picture ran through Westin's mind. Donna, trapped in the limousine at the bottom of the ravine, bleeding to death, choking, drowning, burning to death...

"Dammit, shoot!"

"Donna—"

"She's not in there! You let those sons of bitches get away, that's more to come after you, Donna and your kids."

Westin thought again of killing his wife. He also thought of having this whole job to do over again, except that this time it wouldn't be Donna in the gangsters' hands, it would be Ricky and Fiona.

He remembered to let his breath out as his finger closed on the trigger of the M-14.

DONNA WESTIN CAME UP the stairs as Bolan finished the message. She had on a shirt three sizes too large for her. Over one arm she carried a pair of equally outsize jeans, and in the other hand she held the Hi-Power.

Bolan covered her while she finished dressing. He saw no signs of life on the farm, but thought he heard rifle fire in the distance. When it came a second time, he was sure, and also knew the direction. The ambush party had gone into action.

"Good guys or bad guys?" Donna asked. With clothes on she looked and sounded almost normal, if you ignored the bare feet and the Hi-Power stuck in the waist of the jeans.

"Both," Bolan said briefly. "I left a couple of friends to cut off the road downhill."

"And uphill?"

"Another friend." Not knowing if any live enemies might be in hearing, he didn't mention the helicopter. "Now we'd better get moving."

Donna looked at the cars, but Bolan shook his head. She frowned. "Look, I don't know who you are, but I can't hike cross-country barefoot."

"Borrow something." Bolan pointed to a dead hardman who wore purple cross-trainers. Donna gulped, then knelt and began unlacing the dead man's shoes. They were also too large for her, but when Bolan pointed toward the trees she followed.

"Wouldn't we join up with your friends faster if we drove?" she said when the farm was out of sight.

"We would," he replied, "but we'd also give the bad guys more warning. Easier for them to lay an ambush themselves or follow us."

Bolan was even more worried about a man who might still not be a bad guy but certainly wasn't answering his radio like a good one. The Shadow seemed to have dropped off the face of the earth. Once Donna Westin was safe, Bolan decided, he was coming back uphill and going over Stormgren Farm with a fine-tooth comb. If that gave the Shadow a shot at him, well, then they'd know where they stood, and there'd be no innocents in the line of fire.

Invisible above the treetops, a column of black greasy smoke curled up into the sky to merge with the grayness of the clouds.

ETTORE MANGNANI DIED about the time Donna Westin walked upstairs. Tom Westin's bullets hit Lucco Contamine, the driver, in the left shoulder, neck and head. He died instantly.

His muscles, however, spasmed as he died. He jerked the wheel hard to the right and stepped on the gas. A worse combination of movements would have been impossible.

The Lincoln lurched forward and to the right, a course that took it over the edge of the cliff. It went ninety feet straight down, and by the time it reached the bottom it was falling nose-first.

As a result it compressed its twenty feet of length into something less than half that. It also ruptured its gas tank, which cremated the dead and dying inside and sent burning gasoline floating down the stream.

The second Lincoln's driver hit the gas, too, when he heard the shots. He was around the curve and had a straight stretch of downhill road ahead of him. He thought he might get away, and he might have been right, because Tom Westin was too busy admiring his first hits to try for more.

Al Torstensson didn't waste time shouting at Westin. He went to work himself. His M-1 Garand wasn't as precise a weapon as Westin's M-14, but it was enough for the other Mangnani Lincoln.

A bullet in the left front tire made the car slew violently, fishtail and come to a stop with the back wheels over the edge of the cliff. Two hardmen in the front seat leaped out. Torstensson took out one, Westin the other.

The loss of weight in the front seats unbalanced the Lincoln. It tipped up and slid backward over the cliff and exploded.

Torstensson saw Westin start to shake.

"Don't freeze up now, pal."

"Donna..."

"She wasn't in those Lincolns, I'm telling you."

"If she was—"

"She wasn't. But she might find *you* dead if you don't help me keep those boys' heads down." The two hardmen who'd leaped free in time had guessed where their enemies were and found hiding places. Torstensson had a pretty good idea of where they were hiding and doubted they could move against him and Westin without being spotted.

But it would be handy if Mike Belasko didn't have any loose ends to tie up at the farm. Better still, if he could bring Donna Westin along, it would put some stuffing back in her husband.

Tom Westin had done damned well for an amateur in his first fight. But he was still an amateur, and the rest of this job looked like one for the professionals.

BOLAN MAINTAINED radio silence until he and Donna were halfway to the ambush site. He felt sorry for Tom Westin, sweating out the possibility that he'd killed his wife because of a friend's mistake. He didn't feel sorry enough to give the Shadow any chance of overhearing the radio call.

By the time Bolan was far enough into the trees to risk calling, he could hear a low-intensity firefight going on. The M-1 would fire every half minute or so, and twice Bolan heard a pistol shot.

Al Torstensson was still in action, and at least one hardman. Bolan hoped the silent M-14 didn't mean that Donna had escaped from the Capezzis only to end up a widow.

Above the trees Bolan now saw smoke beginning to dissipate, but enough for one, even two burning cars. He found a clearing and called.

"Al, the farm's clear, Donna's with me—"

"Oh, God!"

"Shut up, Tom," Torstensson's voice came back. "Thanks for the word, Mike. Where are you?"

Bolan hesitated. Torstensson caught the hint. "Can you let Donna make it in to us on her own while you cut to the left? That way you'll flank a couple of bad guys who don't seem to know they're licked."

It would save time to let the woman make her own way to the rendezvous. Saving time could have them all out of there before the Shadow carried out the next stage of his plan.

But the Shadow's plan might include following them, watching for the moment when Bolan was no longer protecting Donna. The warrior studied the forest around them, saw no signs of pursuit, but knew that proved very little. In this kind of temperate-zone rain forest, even second-growth, a man could be invisible at fifty yards.

"I'd rather bring her all the way in. She doesn't know the woods—"

"Mr. Belasko, I've been camping with Tom more often than you've been to bars!"

"Sorry. Okay. I'd rather bring her all the way in. The bad guys could move around." Bolan hoped Torstensson would fill in for himself what the Executioner didn't want to say on the radio.

"We'll try to keep them hot for you."

"If they're cold when I get there, I won't complain."

Bolan hooked the radio onto his harness and made a quick weapons inspection. Donna Westin watched him closely.

"You're awfully casual about this, aren't you?" she asked as the warrior finished a minor adjustment to the Weatherby's scope.

"If you do what I've done for as long as I've done it, you have two choices," Bolan said. "Casual or crazy."

"Which are you?"

"You mean, which do I *think* I am? You're not going to take my unsupported word on this, are you?"

She managed a faint smile. "And me a lawyer? No, but you seem safe somehow, in spite of all the guns."

"I'm not safe to everybody, Donna."

He slung the Weatherby and scanned the trees again for signs of the Shadow. Finding nothing, he held out his hand. "Let's move."

They covered the last half mile to the ambush site by a roundabout route. Bolan stopped several times to backtrack, holding the Weatherby ready for a snap shot. After the third time he did this, Donna was frowning.

"Is somebody following us, or are you just taking precautions?"

"Precautions."

"But the farm's clear, isn't it?"

"Maybe. Even if it is, there could be people from the limos Al didn't see."

"Okay. I won't complain, seeing as how it's my rear end on the line along with yours."

There was nothing wrong with Donna Westin's rear end, or any other part of her, including her nerves. Come to think of it, her husband was a fairly tough specimen, too, considering what he'd done.

Nobody appeared on Bolan's trail, and nothing changed about the firefight, except that the pistol shots were down to one a minute. The Executioner wondered what the hardmen were doing besides keeping their courage up. If that was all they were doing, they were heading for a sudden crisis of confidence the minute they fired their last round.

The hardmen nearly had a last chance when Tom Westin looked over his shoulder and saw his wife standing by a fir tree. He jumped up, forgetting his rifle, his enemies, his cover and concealment. He ran to her, whirled her off her feet and hugged her so tightly that she squealed.

Torstensson shouted, "Get down, you idiots!" and tried to grab Westin's ankle. He got Donna's instead; she kicked at his hand, hit his M-1 and it went flying.

Bolan hit the dirt, rolling into position and aiming the Weatherby down the slope. He'd just got a good sight when the two hardmen made a break for it. One he took down with a head shot, but the other zigged when Bolan expected him to zag. He made it to cover with nothing worse than a shoulder wound, and his gun still in hand.

"Cover me," Bolan said briefly. He slung the Weatherby and hooked the shoulder-stocked Beretta to his belt. "And give me that rope, Al."

Torstensson tossed him the sixty-foot rope, and the Executioner raced off downhill, trying to move without cracking a twig or rustling a leaf. The care might be wasted against the last hardman, but not against the Shadow.

Bolan crossed the road, looped the rope around a stump, then rappeled down the cliff to a ledge he'd spotted from above. Retrieving the rope, he crawled along the ledge until he was below and slightly to the right of the hardman's cover.

"Our friend still in place?" he whispered into the radio.

"No sign that he's left. No more shots, either."

"Okay. I'll try to take him alive."

"I'd rather you didn't take chances, Mike."

"It's a bigger chance not being able to ask any questions."

Torstensson didn't argue; he knew Bolan was right. Instead he sent three rounds from the M-1 in the hardman's general direction as Bolan used fingers and toes to creep up to the level of the road.

As he found a firm perch at road level, he raised the Beretta, took off the safety and shouted, "Freeze! Throw out your gun and come out with your hands up. Do anything else, and you're history."

Bolan heard the hardman cough, then give something like a sigh of relief. A Walther automatic came flying out of the bushes, skidding almost into Bolan's hands.

"Now you."

The bushes wavered, as if moved by a high wind. A barrel-chested young man climbed slowly into view, mud and blood staining his clothes. He held one hand to a bloody shoulder and was plucking dead needles off his designer jeans with the other.

The next moment all his worries about wounds, appearance or anything else came to an end. From off to Bolan's left, a G-3 rattled out a quick burst. The hardman's head flew apart, and his chest gaped open.

Bolan dived across the road, landing in the same mud where the hardman had lain. Bullets from the G-3 followed him every foot of the way, kicking up gravel behind him.

The Executioner studied the opposite side of the valley as well as he could without leaving cover. As he'd expected, the Shadow could be hiding anywhere. He fired two rounds from the Weatherby into two of the most likely hiding places, just to prove that he'd received the intended message.

The Shadow replied with three single shots. The warrior wasted no more time, but hurled himself up the slope toward his friends.

Again bullets from the G-3 followed him, but this time the Shadow was shooting to kill. The trees that hid Bolan half the time and deflected the bullets the rest, his own evasive tactics and a good bit of luck got him halfway up the slope unscathed.

At that point the shooting stopped as suddenly as if Bolan had become invisible. The warrior put the Shadow to one final test. He stood up in plain sight and walked the rest of the way to his friends without trying to hide.

No bullet came. The Shadow had met and passed the final test. The Executioner was his target, and no one else.

Now it was Bolan's turn to face the test the Shadow had set him.

But first he had to explain to the others why he was going to head off into the Olympic Peninsula on the Shadow's trail.

Alone.

19

Mack Bolan lay half-hidden behind an exposed root of a medium-sized Douglas fir. The Weatherby was braced between the root and a rock he'd wedged in place.

With his binoculars the warrior scanned the opposite hillside. If the Shadow wanted a shot at the helicopter, he'd have to be somewhere on that hillside. If he was, Bolan was betting he'd show himself to fire.

A day had passed since the battle at Stormgren Farm and the Shadow's changing sides. Bolan had spent the past twenty-four hours on the man's trail, a trail that a Boy Scout could have followed. But now they were inside the Olympic National Forest, where it would be more difficult to track the Shadow but much more necessary.

The tourist season was getting under way; backpackers would be swarming into the park and the Shadow might decide to take a hostage.

Above and behind the Executioner came the sound of rotors. He shifted slightly to watch the Huey sliding down out of the overcast sky. From the sling under the fuselage dangled the olive-drab pack that held Bolan's resupply of equipment.

His radio fizzed, and he heard Monty Pelham's voice.

"Ready to drop. All clear?"

"As far as I can see."

Pelham grunted something in reply, then the sling started to descend.

Both the shots and the strikes were soundless, but Bolan saw the results clearly. One window in the Huey turned white with starred cracks, and he thought he saw a couple of holes appear in the aluminum of the main door.

"Dump it, Monty!"

Pelham didn't need the Executioner's order. The sling's load had been packed with just this situation in mind. When Pelham released the cable, the load plummeted thirty feet, hit, bounced six feet and rolled into the bush.

Bolan didn't waste time worrying about retrieving it. He saw movement on that slope he'd been studying for so long, and was gluing his eye to the Weatherby's sight as the slung load crunched to a stop.

The moving figure wore a blacksuit and carried what looked more like a G-3 than anything else. Bolan's finger squeezed the trigger, the Weatherby's firing pin fell on a cartridge and a heavy slug blasted across the valley. But the Shadow ducked behind a tree just as Bolan committed himself to firing.

A moment later he popped out again, the G-3 to his shoulder. It bucked, and 7.62 mm rounds chewed bark out of Bolan's tree. As he'd done before, the Shadow seemed to be firing high. A bad habit, or a deliberate trick to keep Bolan on his trail?

Certainly he could have taken out the Huey. Bolan decided that the Shadow was still playing games and resumed his study of the hillside. He wasn't optimistic; ten feet up-slope from the Shadow's tree lay brush thick enough to deflect a howitzer shell, let alone the Weatherby's rounds. But keeping the Shadow pinned down for a while would at least keep him from trying for Bolan's supplies.

The Executioner also realized that the standoff would keep *him* from retrieving his own supplies.

He looked at his watch. With this overcast sky, it would be dark in about three hours. Then he could move to retrieve his supplies without being seen. Probably not without being heard, but the Shadow's lack of wilderness experience would make him less effective at night. Bolan would have his supplies by midnight, then a real advantage over the Shadow, who had only what he'd taken from Stormgren Farm.

Except that it was hard to tell what that might be, because the Shadow had torched the farmhouse before he left. If the man had planned properly, he might also have cached a couple of weeks' dried rations, extra ammunition, a first-aid kit and more weapons somewhere deep in the park. Probably somewhere that offered a good place for ambushing the Executioner.

As the cloudy sky finally kept its promise of rain, Bolan used the deteriorating visibility to retreat from his post. He thought he saw movement, but heard no shots.

In ten minutes he had the sling. In another ten he was heading for the densest patch of undergrowth he could find. The full load was nearly fifty pounds, so

Bolan knew he couldn't help leaving a trail. But he didn't want to stop, break it down and still be relaying it into a hiding place when darkness fell.

The Shadow might not be good at tracking prey by sound, but anybody could get lucky. The best way of keeping the Shadow's luck bad would be to make no sound.

By nightfall Bolan was snuggled down under a poncho, weapons and radio at hand. He was confident that he'd made the right decision to trail the Shadow on his own, confident that he was a better woodsman and that this tactic would keep the Shadow farther from innocent people. He wasn't so confident that the outcome of this hunt wouldn't be decided by pure luck.

BY THE TIME Bolan picked up the Shadow's trail the next day, it was early afternoon. By now he recognized the prints of the man's boots, and there were plenty of them to recognize. Almost too many to believe, in fact, considering how hard it rained the previous night. Was it possible two men could be in the area wearing the same boots?

A mile farther on, Bolan was satisfied he was still trailing only one man. A man who must have left that trail deliberately to draw his pursuer on.

He scanned the land ahead, but without results.

By midafternoon the warrior had followed the trail into the bottom of a steep-sided valley. It wound up into the mountains, and a rain-swollen stream roared past Bolan's feet.

In the distance he could see a cloud of mist rising from the valley. It was so localized that he knew it had to be a waterfall. He checked his location on the map and learned that he'd guessed right. The valley dead-ended in a vertical cliff of nearly two hundred feet, with a waterfall pouring over the edge.

Bolan knew that he had to go far enough up the valley to remind the Shadow that he was still being followed. Even better would be far enough to draw fire. Best of all would be far enough to get off a shot of his own.

The Executioner lightly oiled the barrel of the Weatherby, then checked the bore for water and debris. He adjusted the sights for the shorter range he expected in the valley, then started to climb the rocks beside the stream.

AT A SNAIL'S PACE it took Bolan half an hour to get well up into the valley. As he advanced, he saw the Shadow's footprints plain wherever the ground was level enough to show them. Bolan himself stayed as close to concealment as possible.

That wasn't always as close as he liked. The combination of underbrush, trees and rocks changed with every bend in the valley. Sometimes a platoon could have hidden within ten feet of Bolan. At other times a chicken would have been conspicuous. It didn't help to know that the valley could at any moment turn into a shooting gallery, with Bolan as the duck.

That thought came back several times until it triggered one of Bolan's instincts. It was the one that let him tell where taking risks stopped and foolhardiness began. Foolhardiness, he decided, began another hundred yards up the valley. There the valley sides grew too steep to climb. If he went past that point, he'd not only be in the shooting gallery, he wouldn't be able to get out of it.

Fifty yards farther on, Bolan started his climb out of the valley. He was crossing the stream when he saw a flicker of movement high on the left-hand side. He froze and waited for the movement to stop or reveal a target.

It stopped, but in a position to show that it was some sort of animal. From the color, Bolan guessed it was a deer, maybe a doe with a fawn heading for greener feeding higher up.

Bolan slipped across the stream and began to climb. Here the valley sides weren't quite steep enough for him to need handholds. He preferred to keep both hands for the Weatherby and take his time finding good footholds.

The valley sides rose nearly a hundred and fifty feet from the streambed. By now Bolan could see the upper part of the waterfall. A number of warped, blackened trees jutted out from the vertical rock faces on either side of the falls.

The warrior was halfway up the valley side when he saw the animal moving again. Another minute, another ten feet, and Bolan saw what it was.

It wasn't a deer, with a fawn or without one. It was a huge mountain lion, sleek, obviously well fed, moving with an almost sinuous grace. In moments it would be in a position where it could spring down on the Executioner.

Bolan had heard that mountain lions seldom attacked human beings unless they were threatened. He hadn't heard how to keep two hundred pounds of predatory feline from feeling threatened. He decided to start by not looking directly at it. That would avoid eye contact, which some animals took as a challenge.

It would also let him look at the Weatherby as he slowly shifted it into position for a quick shot. Bolan saw that everything was well with his rifle and cautiously stretched one leg for a better foothold, then froze.

A blacksuited figure had appeared from behind a tree beside the waterfall. Kneeling, he was bringing his G-3 into firing position.

Uphill, Bolan heard the big cat growling, and its tail lashed a path through damp leaves. It was getting ready to attack.

With a minimum of luck, Bolan would get off one shot. Counting on only that minimum, which should it be? The Shadow or the mountain lion?

The Shadow, Bolan decided, had to be counting on the mountain lion. Otherwise he wouldn't have exposed himself so completely.

That meant optimism about his opponent doing what was expected of him. A common kind of optimism, and as fatal as it was common.

Trying to move slowly and ignore the growls, Bolan brought the Weatherby up from the grass. The moment he had a firm two-handed grip, he rolled, sat up, threw the big rifle to his shoulder and fired.

The blacksuited figure collapsed. From uphill the mountain lion screamed. Two hundred pounds of tawny fury soared toward Bolan as he rolled again.

His roll only took him ten feet, but he'd started it just as the cat leaped. By the time the animal realized his prey was moving, it was too late. He twisted in midair but only succeeded in landing in a sprawl. On the steep slope that was more than even a cat's agility and claws could handle.

Bolan watched the mountain lion roll down the valley and into the stream. As the big cat hit the water, the warrior swung around so that he could watch both feline and human opponents at the same time.

The Shadow seemed to have vanished. Then Bolan saw a black-clad form, arms and legs outflung, sprawled in one of the dead trees sticking out beside the waterfall.

The mountain lion thrashed its way out of the water, growling furiously. Bolan kept the sights on it as it lashed its tail and clawed up fist-sized tufts of grass.

"Come on, pussycat," he muttered under his breath. "I don't want an argument with you. So move it!"

The cat seemed equally reluctant to leave and to charge. Bolan looked at the Shadow again. One arm was moving feebly. The man was still alive, which meant still fighting.

The Weatherby roared, and a bullet sparked off a rock ten feet to the left of the mountain lion. The animal jumped so high that Bolan thought he'd hit it with a ricochet. It then let out a screaming roar that echoed around the valley, and loped away downstream. Bolan waited until the mountain lion was out of sight before he started climbing again.

He had to detour around a nearly vertical pitch on the last part of his climb. So it was nearly ten minutes before he reached the Shadow.

The hitter was lying on his back among the branches of the tree. At first sight he looked unhurt, but Bolan quickly saw that the right thigh and lower torso of his blacksuit were soaked with blood. Also, a jagged stub of branch had speared his left leg.

Bolan started uncoiling the climbing rope. The man didn't deserve to die the slow death of a belly wound, caught in the dead tree like a fly in a spider web.

"Hey, Executioner..." The voice was barely audible above the roar of the falls, but the words were clear.

"You know who I am?"

"Never much doubt. Knew it after the Tong hit. Not many men...working for the Families...get to see Mack the Bastard in action...."

There was nothing to say to that. Or if there was, Bolan couldn't think of it.

"Why?" was all he could say. He'd seldom wanted to find out why one of the criminals he killed had done something. But he'd never before had an ally and enemy combined in one man.

"Simple enough." The Shadow coughed so hard for so long that Bolan expected the tree to break under him. By the time he stopped coughing, blood was flowing out of his mouth.

"Simple," he said, so quietly that Bolan had to strain to hear him. "With you helping me there'd be twice as much mess...in the Seattle Families. Then...with me Don Pietro's heir and...your head for credentials...who else to run Seattle?''

"And Don Pietro's money?''

"Re-re-member. Million dollars for your head—'' Another coughing fit ended the speech.

It made sense to Bolan as he paid out the rope. The man who'd taken the Executioner would have the voice of half the Commission. He'd also have a million dollars, plus whatever he could persuade Don Pietro and the heirs of the two dead Dons to produce.

Bolan still wouldn't have trusted the Shadow to keep his hands off the daughters' money forever. That he was shrewder than the average mafioso didn't make him less greedy.

"Can you tie this rope around yourself if I throw one end down?'' Bolan asked. The Shadow moved his head, maybe nodding or maybe just relieving cramped neck muscles.

"All right.'' Bolan finished making a loop in the end of the rope and started letting it down.

As he did, the Shadow's right arm twitched again, then curved up toward his belt. Toward his Hi-Power.

Bolan dropped flat, drawing the Desert Eagle as he did. But he didn't need to shoot, even if the Shadow had been making a last effort. The dying man tilted as his arm came up, and slid off the trunk onto branches too light to bear his weight. They bent and he slid off into space.

In silence he plunged two hundred feet into the mist at the base of the falls. Their roar drowned out any splash.

Bolan holstered his weapon, stood and began to wind up the rope. He wasn't sorry the Shadow was dead, but he was glad he'd been able to ask those last few questions. The Seattle Families were down but not out, and the first step to putting them down was Don Pietro's death.

For Donna Westin's sake, Bolan wouldn't have minded sparing her father. But the old Don had lived too long and might have too many hidden resources to make that safe.

The best the Executioner could do was strike silently and anonymously, so that Donna could never be sure what happened to her father.

"MORNING, STRIKER. Did I wake you?"

"No, Hal. I didn't crash yet."

"If you're planning to hit Don Pietro—"

"You know the value of time as well as I do. If I move in while the Britos are still off balance—"

"Don Pietro's dead," the big Fed said flatly.

"Capezzi soldiers?"

"Heart attack last night. His *consigliere* came in this morning with their files on the Silent Brotherhood and a load of other stuff. Good stuff, most of it. He told us something that probably explains Don Pietro's heart attack."

"What's that?"

"Your late partner, Leon Fieromosca, a.k.a. the Shadow, was Don Pietro's illegitimate son."

Bolan wasn't completely surprised. The voices had been a bit too much alike for coincidence.

"Well, Don Pietro was badly surprised when he learned that his son was dead. Fatally surprised."

"Did the Shadow know?"

"The *consigliere* didn't say."

It didn't really matter. Father and son were both gone where they could do no more harm.

"Then I guess we have things pretty well wound up—"

"Hal, there's a lot about this that isn't anywhere *near* wound up."

Bolan started listing items: telling Gunny Cullom that Corporal Goss had finally died like a Marine, and asking him about anyone else in the Corps who might have a lead on the Silent Brotherhood; covering Al Torstensson's and Monty Pelham's tracks, so they stayed out of trouble with the police; making the Zorinos an offer they couldn't refuse, to go out of business instead of trying to pick up where the three wrecked Families had left off; getting a good lead on the Silent Brotherhood, with both Sam Brito and Corporal Goss dead; making sure that the Blue Lily Tong didn't come after Lieutenant Thanh and his Viets. In fact, making sure that there *was* no Blue Lily Tong to come after anybody.

"Okay, okay." Bolan could practically hear Brognola holding up his hands to stop the flow of words. "I give in. You can hang out in Seattle until you're good and ready to leave, for all I care. Need anything?"

"Not right now. I'll be in touch."

After Brognola hung up, it occurred to Bolan that he'd left out one final project. A gallant young lady by the name of Gloria needed a new start in life, and preferably a new identity.

It wasn't always true that the end of every evil was the beginning of a new good. But it was beginning to look that way about the nightmare in the Northwest.

That thought let the Executioner sleep in, for one of the few times in his life.

From the publishers of AGENTS, an action-driven new miniseries focusing on the war against drugs.

CODE ZERO

D. A. HODGMAN

The action gets hot when CENTAC—an elite tactical unit of the DEA—receives CODE ZERO. The license to track and terminate, CODE ZERO is the DEA's answer to the drug cartels.

In Book 1: SPEEDBALL, DEA agents are massacred in a furious firefight, but one is kept alive and taken hostage. Agent Harry Wolfe will stop at nothing to rescue her as he battles against the rampaging gunmen.